Encounters

stories by Michael Trussler

NEWEST PRESS

Library and Archives Canada Cataloguing in Publication
Trussler, Michael Lloyd, 1960-

Encounters / Michael Trussler.

(Nunatak fiction)

ISBN-13: 978-1-897126-00-4
ISBN-10: 1-897126-00-X

I. Title. II. Series.

PS8639.R89E53 2006   C813'.6   C2006-902992-X

Editor for the press: Thomas Wharton
Cover and interior design: Ruth Linka
Cover image: istockphoto.com
Author photo: Amy Snider

 Canada Council **Conseil des Arts**   Canadian Patrimoine   edmonton arts council
for the Arts **du Canada**   Heritage canadien

NeWest Press acknowledges the support of the Canada Council for the Arts and the Alberta Foundation for the Arts, and the Edmonton Arts Council for our publishing program. We also acknowledge the financial support of the Government of Canada through the Book Publishing Industry Development Program (BPIDP) for our publishing activities.

NeWest Press
201–8540–109th Street
Edmonton, Alberta, T6G 1E6
(780) 432-9427
www.newestpress.com

To Susan, incomparable friend,
and Annie and Jesse, my children

That's what a human is: a gathering around a perplexity.
— Leonard Cohen, Interview

Table of Contents

People Are Much More Adventurous Now

⁓ The evergreen's blurred enough already, but some of its branches are barely visible behind the plastic Ziploc bag. The fish inside the bag looks as if it's alive—its open eyes meeting yours are so huge—but of course it can't be. The eyes are unusual; very few fish species have faces that join their eyes together on the same plane. The background sky looks scoured, an endless white. In the photo's lower right, the upper tip of a faded telephone pole suggests the ghost of a dragonfly.

He taped the photograph into a large sketchbook, gave it a title in pencil, and closed the book. He wrapped a copy of the photo in Cellophane, placed it inside an envelope, and turned off the lights. It was just after three in the morning, the right time to go.

As always, he drove to the provincial parliament building and parked his car in front of the lake. It was abnormally warm. The legislature's dome glistened behind winter fog. He could hear the geese that gathered to rest in the middle of the lake, two or three flocks that banded together at night. The birds usually appeared as a dark streak across the ice from where he stood, but this time they were hidden beneath the unusual February mist. Earlier that night the moon had been barely visible behind strands of dark sky, reminding him of tight skin behind the run in someone's black nylons.

A few weeks before, when he'd left the car and was about to make his way to the residential side of the street, the stars had offered him a never to be repeated gift. It had been oppressively cold, below minus thirty. He'd just closed the car's door, the metal grinding shut, and the air had held a slight sweetness that could only have come from the stars. He'd been completely alone, the lake hard in front of him, the car's engine cooling down, and the stars had reached out with the gift of their scent that lasted until he'd got to the traffic lights and crossed the street.

It took ten minutes to do what he'd come to do, and then he was back beside the car. He threw a snowball out into the lake, and as always, played some Philip Glass as he drove home. When he turned onto the street that led to where he lived a gargoyle was waiting for him on a street lamp. Covered in mist and wet with the night, the monster's face didn't show. But there it sat, just the same.

The next night it's Saturday. A cluster of friends have been making it a point to go cross-country skiing on Saturday nights, but tonight the snow's too wet. On good nights, they ski for a couple of hours, and then take turns hosting dinner.

This Saturday it's Ester and Marcus' turn to cook, so instead of skiing, everyone's gone directly to their home. A specialist in policing, Marcus has just returned from a consulting trip to Russia, making it inevitable that the meal starts with borsch.

When Marcus had mentioned to one of his colleagues in Moscow that he wanted to take a bust of Lenin home as a souvenir, he'd received an entire case the next day. What he's done tonight is put a miniature bust of Lenin and a small airplane bottle of vodka in front of each place setting as party favours.

Ester had inherited a floral business from her father, and she's expanded from his one store to three. People are much more adventurous now with what they'll buy than they were in her dad's day. Beta fish swim with their trailing baroque fins amongst plants in tall rectangular containers, languid, living ink, one for each guest—Ester's contribution to the table.

"But how are we to get them home?" Yvonne, who teaches in the French Department at the university, protests. "They're tropical fish—won't they die in the cold?"

"I'll have them delivered next week. If you want, I'll have yours dropped off at your office."

When Anika had seen the fish an hour earlier, she'd immediately tensed up.

That morning there'd been another photograph in the mailbox, this time one of a dead fish. She's brought the picture with her, and some of the others, but she doesn't want to show them just yet. She still hasn't told her husband Julian about the packages that started appearing shortly after her third novel had come out, six months earlier. Born in Copenhagen, she'd written her first book in Danish, but has since switched to English.

"Kill the Bach, Ester, no one can eat to Bach," Marcus says.

Of all the people at the table, it's George, Yvonne's husband, who's read Anika's work most closely. His signed copies of her novels are filled with annotations, but he's never spoken much to Anika about what she's written.

The best dish is the salad dressed with pine nuts.

Before they'd sat down to eat, sliding in together on the old church pews Ester had refinished for her large dining room, they'd admired Marcus's newest acquisition, a partial, black and white blueprint of the Lubyanka, former playground of the KGB Scattered throughout the house are original drawings of old prisons. Newgate, the Abbey of Fontevraud, Spandau.

"Tink's quit her music lessons," George tells Anika.

"Tink's his name for Liselle," Yvonne says.

"Because she pouts just like Tinker Bell," George explains. "She's just like her mother. Unless she can do something perfectly, she wants to quit."

"That's the way Ester was on our honeymoon," Marcus says.

Anika's never seen *Peter Pan*. Aware that her knowledge of North American popular culture is minimal at best, she believes that this gap serves her writing well. "What instrument does she play?" she asks.

"The snare drum," George says.

"Liselle plays the violin," Yvonne says.

"Well, she used to."

Ester knows that Yvonne will judge the decorative fish as being an unnecessary indulgence, but, meeting Anika's eyes, she hopes that she will see them for what they are: a small act of slightly unordinary colour and inspiration.

Marcus had been charmed by the Russian habit of toasting.

He'd learned that every social gathering had to have at least three elaborate toasts. And then, if there were more—which happened frequently with Russian police, the total number had to be a multiple of three. Marcus had thanked his guests by going around the table, praising the women first; Yvonne for the wide-eyed beauty of her unrelenting anti-American politics, Anika's spot on ability to make him uncomfortable—he's always respected her for keeping him on his toes—and his wife Ester deserved credit for her aesthetic sense, both at the table and on other, less culinary occasions.

Teasing Julian, Marcus had remarked how grateful they were for his terribly tangled psyche, which had provided Anika with some wonderful material that had enriched all of their bedtime reading; and George invited nothing but respect for his fingernails.

They were glittery with nail polish.

"This was Tink's idea," George had said, "she put it on herself, looks pretty good don't you think?"

Ester's hand had shot across the table when George had spoken, opening up his hands, almost knocking over the glass with his fish in it. She'd caught his wrist, stopping him before he'd ruined the table setting.

Anika has never written about her husband. But Marcus was telling the truth about Yvonne's politics. She'd admitted to Julian and Marcus over cocktails that she was going to attend the march tomorrow. She, along with other peace activists, was going to protest the American decision to invade Iraq. People were invited to bring balloons, placards, anything that would make noise, and they would march from the World War I cenotaph in Victoria Park to the legislature. A few years earlier, Yvonne had joined other people on the Albert Street bridge, drawing the attention of passersby to the bombing of Kosovo.

"I want to offer a toast to Yvonne," Julian announces. He stands, resting one hand on Anika's shoulder, and thanks Yvonne for her political life, knowing full well that Ester, who regularly sends donations to Israel, felt differently about world politics. The best dinner parties, Julian has long felt, involve subdued theatre.

"And I admire you too, Yvonne," Julian continued, "for taking Liselle along with you, letting her know there's more to the world than Regina. When I was her age the only thing I cared about was comic books."

Action heroes hadn't appealed to Julian as much as horror stories. *Tales of Mystery*, anything supernatural. A long forgotten wretch in a business suit, freezing in Bedlam, suddenly passes across Julian's mind.

The man in the comic book had left a bar in the twentieth century, got lost in a snowstorm, and opened a red door that left him in the insane asylum. Stranded in another century, he'd naturally been judged to be mad, and he'd been incarcerated. Julian can still see him huddled in a panel that dripped icicles.

Disappointed that no one's commented on his new antique belt buckle from Moscow, Marcus isn't drunk enough to draw anyone's attention to it, so he tells the table instead that that morning he and Ester had a minor squabble, and Rachel had come into the kitchen and asked him if he needed his suitcase. She'd said that she knew where he kept it in the basement.

"She's only four and she's already got your number," Anika tells him.

How can she do that? Marcus wonders. Anika was looking at Marcus as if she knew about Xenia, but that was impossible. A young police cadet with whom he'd spent the previous Saturday night before he'd flown home Sunday, Xenia had been delightfully embarrassed about her smelly feet and had wanted to have a shower first. But he'd taken her by the wrist and said he wanted her like she was.

Dessert is a tray of fruit that looks as though Jackson Pollock has spray-painted it in chocolate.

"Did you go to Lenin's mausoleum when you were in Moscow?" George asks Marcus.

"Too busy—I work when I go to Russia. I can't waste time standing in lineups."

"I can't imagine that the wait is very long these days," Julian says. "Whatever happened to the Left?"

"Marcus brought back some cognac. Let's go into the living room by the fire and I'll pour some," Ester says.

"Ester, can we have the brandy here? There's something curious I want to show everyone. And I need the table. It will only take a few minutes," Anika says, going to get her bag.

She clears a space and puts a framed photograph on the table.

The 5x7 black and white picture is divided in half by a line. The top, a kind of dreamscape that holds a woman's face, trees empty of leaves—everything amidst a thick, gradually darkening sky—but underneath is a different world; everything's reversed, upside down. Trees in the top half of the photograph are reflected upside down. Their branches, reaching downward instead of rising up, appear to be roots that grow down into fully-grown nether trees. There's another face mirrored below, this one with clearer features, and a long, terrible throat hanging precisely beneath the blurry face mirrored above. The face below looks like a fresh corpse. Above, the woman's spirit only just lifting; beneath, the world of exactly wrinkled skin, the terrible black nostrils, hair caught in a breeze.

"If you turn it the other side up, you can see it's obviously a reflection on the roof of a car," Anika says.

"It looks like it was taken at the Centre of the Arts."

"I think so too."

"You've taken up photography and didn't tell us," says George.

"Anika, what's going on?" Julian wants to know, completely uncertain as to why he's beginning to feel afraid.

"Look closely," Anika says. "There's something wrong with the picture: the faces aren't identical; they're two different women."

"Anika, where did you get this picture?"

"It's simple. Several months ago it showed up in our mailbox. No name, nothing, just a framed picture wrapped in newspaper. And then about six weeks later, this one."

Inside a Barbie picture frame is a small figurine, Batgirl, lying face up on top of a naked female torso. Batgirl's feet rest on what presumably is the adult woman's pubic hair, it's hard to tell; far off, way up beyond the stomach curving to the side, are blurred breasts. The picture ends there.

"Anika, why didn't you tell me about this before?" Julian asks.

"And this morning a dead fish in a plastic bag," Anika says, looking at her husband. "But this one came in Cellophane, no frame," she adds, moving her drink, and putting the picture down so the others can see. "Let's see what Marcus thinks."

Everyone looks to Marcus, expectant.

"Knowing you, I assume that you haven't contacted the police," he says.

"Of course not—they appear to be gifts."

"Why do you think that they're for you?" Marcus asks.

"Because each one has come with my author's photograph from my last book. Whoever is sending me these pictures cuts out my picture from the dust jacket. I guess that means that at least I've made three more sales."

"Any messages? A note or something?"

"Nope."

"Ever notice anyone strange when you do a reading?"

Anika laughs.

"No, nobody strange. Sorry, Marcus, I couldn't help it. It's not as though I pack the house when I do a reading, that's all."

"Do you get threatening phone calls?"

"Just from my sister. Honestly, Marcus, I don't think that there's anything dangerous happening here; I only brought them because I wanted to find out what all of you thought."

"I think they're dreadful," says Yvonne. "I don't think they're gifts at all. They're an invasion of your privacy."

"And what doesn't invade my privacy?"

"Marcus, what kind of person does something like this?" asks Julian. "What's going on here?"

"Anika, you say that this started when?"

"A month or so after I published *The Weatherman's Day Off.*"

"Doesn't a man kill his wife in that book?"

"Depends on how you read it. But I think you're on the wrong track. I don't think there's anything criminal going on at all."

"What do you think the pictures are for then?"

"I really don't know. That's why I brought them here. I wanted to find out what everybody thought about them."

"Why would anyone want you to see a dead fish?"

"Marcus, do you think they're threats?" asks George.

"Probably not a threat per se; usually threats come with a note."

"Maybe someone doesn't like my novels," Anika says.

"He knows where you live, Anika. That should concern you," Marcus says.

"Of course it concerns me, but why are you so certain it's a man?"

"That's simple," Yvonne offers. "A woman would never take pictures like those."

"It's probably a man," Marcus says, "but Yvonne, before you get on a high horse, the person who's doing this isn't all that different from you."

"I hope you brought home two bottles of cognac, Marcus," Anika says. "Yvonne wants another sip. Me too. What's that supposed to mean?"

"What I mean," Marcus says, "is that neither Yvonne or the photographer is content to just let things be."

"But that's apples and oranges. Wanting to stop American imperialism isn't the same thing as delivering sordid pictures to a woman's home."

"Perhaps not. But compared to most people, you're involved in abnormal behaviour. You're stepping outside of everyday life. And that's what the photographer's doing too."

"Stop right there. Politics *is* everyday life."

"No it isn't. For people like us, politics is an abstraction. As I was saying, you feel compelled to intervene in things beyond your daily affairs. Just extend what you do and not so far along the spectrum you'll find this fellow with his camera."

"That's psychobabble Marcus," Julian says. "I want to know whether we should call the police."

"If they continue, most definitely."

"Anika, do you think that whoever gives you these pictures is one of your fans?" Ester asks.

"I wouldn't go that far."

"Maybe you should take them to a photo lab. Find out if anyone's brought in a film for these photographs. Or you could check out the bookstores, see if anyone's been buying your books more than one at a time."

"I'm not Sherlock Holmes. And it's bad taste for a writer to ask about her books in a bookstore."

"Anyway, he must have his own dark room," says Julian. "The one of the woman had to be fiddled with."

"Maybe he's hoping that you'll choose one of the photos for the cover of your next book," George says, "or maybe he's trying to spruce up your study. You have to admit that right now it's pretty austere."

"You're not taking this seriously," Yvonne says. "George, this is frightening."

"Do you think it's somebody you know?" Ester asks.

Anika looks around the table, and says, "no." Then she makes her toast in drunken Danish, telling her friends she loves them, but castigates them too. Their reactions to the photographs had been disappointing. She praises Liselle for George's fingernails, but, because of the Danish, Liselle is the only word the others understand.

"What was that about Liselle?" Yvonne asks.

"Shhh," Anika tells her.

The Weatherman's Day Off was about a forensic climatologist with a narrow mustache and rimless glasses whom the police had engaged in their efforts to find a suspect for the killing—execution style behind the skull—of several horses. Not race horses, just ordinary ones used for recreation. They'd died in their stalls, and their killer always left a photograph of the horse taken from when it had been alive. Because the pictures had been shot outdoors with a high power telephoto lens and usually showed cloud patterns, the police had gone to Anika's character for his meteorological analysis, hoping to pin down when the pictures had been taken.

Reading the novel, the photographer felt as though something had slammed him hard, as if he'd been standing on ice and had just been bodychecked from behind. It had been the sentences that Anika had written about the dead horses abandoned on the floors of their stables that had done the shoving. He'd never met this writer who understood so well how the horses would haunt their photos after they'd been shot. Because the novel's images were secondary to its plot, he decided that its author needed to discover a surprise where she wouldn't expect to find one. Images, he knew, are more lyrical, and more exacting, than words.

He hadn't planned on sending more than one photograph, but then he started taking pictures with Anika in mind.

Working with pictures that had a specific destination had made him shed constraints; working with his lens made the old boundaries disappear. It didn't matter if she simply tossed them into the garbage.

The way the world looked was irresistible.

When it got colder Saturday night, two black garbage bags shriveled in an alley. Covered with the recent frost, they looked like contorted bodies cast out of their ancient bog. He drove back to the street and parked his car, then got his equipment and returned to the garbage bags.

But he didn't take their picture.

Photos that needed words were useless. Pictures, the ones that worked, took place beneath the mind's quick simplicity, its peculiar addiction for making comparisons, its mistaken belief that narrative could contain experience. He nailed the rubber mask to a telephone pole, worked at it, fixed the iguana beneath it, poured gasoline over everything, took out his camera, set the gas alight, and shot two rolls of film.

On their walk home, Anika and Julian follow a path in the snow across a vacant lot. The slightly winding set of footprints makes Anika think of the scar from a mastectomy.

"I'm worried about those photographs," Julian says, walking slightly behind. "You should have told me about them before. Why didn't you?"

"Because you'd worry about it."

"If another one arrives, I want you to phone the police."

"Okay," says Anika, though she has no intention of doing so.

"I'm burping fancy cognac and pine nuts."

"Keep that up, and you'll attract animals."

"I'm going to sit up tonight and see if that bastard comes by."

"No, you're not, Anika has other plans for you when we get home."

"I'm serious, Anika."

"Just you wait."

Later that night, Anika gets out of bed, bathes, puts her bust of Lenin in a clear, plastic bag, gets a small hammer and, not wanting to demolish the piece utterly, gently chips off Lenin's beard. You could still tell who it was. It needs something else, but she can't think of what to add to the bag, so she hides it away in her desk. When she comes up with a good idea, she'll put the bag in the mailbox for her secret gift-giver. One good deed deserves another.

Maybe she could put some coloured toothpicks in with Lenin, but she decides that that won't work. A chess piece would be too obvious. A paragraph from the novel she's working on? Her hands are dry so she rubs them with her favourite scented lotion and goes back to bed. Without his glasses, Julian seems tinier somehow.

It takes a few weeks, but eventually the burning mask shows up. Anika shows it to no one.

Her one mistake occurs the night she puts the little bag with the broken bust of Lenin in her mailbox. She's added three things: a small fake sunflower, this sentence on a piece of paper, and the claws she's cut from a bird that had broken its neck against her living room window that morning.

Although she doesn't know it at the time this response makes the photographs stop, and she isn't surprised to find out how much she grows to miss them. She writes three more novels, but nothing ever again shows up in her mailbox. Reviewers note and sometimes criticize how her later work is more fragmented and lyrical. For the next long while she'll scan people at book signings and readings, looking for the photographer, but gets nowhere.

The Saturday dinner parties continue, but except for the one during which she showed the photos it becomes hard for her to keep them apart in her memory. A good researcher, she eventually travels to Latvia, the Ukraine, and Turkey as groundwork for a collection of short stories on the sex trade arising from the economic collapse of Eastern Europe.

Many years later she'll include the pictures along with everything else as an endowment to the university's ongoing archive dedicated to local writers. And this is their final destination, where they'll stay, each one a miniature dam, each holding back its own secret past, each one holding back a lake that may as well be shattered glass.

My Husband Once

⏤ My husband once tore a strip of cotton from a T-shirt and wore it as a blindfold to a costume party. He was pretending to be someone facing a firing squad. Even though he knew that the trip would take over an hour, he insisted on wearing the blindfold all the way from our apartment to the party, which was held in a warehouse downtown. We had to take a bus and then transfer to the subway, and all the while I held his hand and guided him. Up and down dirty, dangerous steps—it had been raining that night—through turnstiles, along the street. Marc spent the entire party blindfolded. People made sure he had beer. While I was dancing I saw someone I didn't know sit down and flash her boobs at him. Poor man, he missed the whole thing. He must have cheated and lowered the blindfold a few times, at least when he went to the washroom—but only when we were making our way home did he take the blindfold off for good. When we got off the bus he suggested I try it on, which I did. It was spooky and fun, and I can still remember all the wetness in the air that night. After guiding me carefully for a few minutes, and making sure that I didn't slip on the grass, he then walked me straight into a parked car. It felt like I'd broken my shins. Granted we were both drunk, and granted he said he was sorry, and granted we've been married now for seventeen years, and although he's never given me any reason to doubt him, I realized even then that he was trying to tell me that I wasn't supposed to put my faith in him.

He'd worn a long white shirt that he'd found in a thrift shop. It was originally part of a tuxedo. While I was putting on my makeup, he'd taken a red magic marker to the back of the shirt, staining in bullet exit wounds—but he'd left the front of the shirt a pristine, immaculate white. He'd worn a piece of cardboard around his neck on which he'd outlined the details of his crime. I went to the party as a high-school cheerleader who'd been bitten late one starless night and become a vampire. Pompoms, a football jersey that doubled as very short skirt, bloody fangs. We couldn't believe it when they announced the prize for the best costume and neither of us had won.

They gave the prize, a real crystal ball, to a belly dancer. I wouldn't mind talking to her now, and finding out what kind of future has happened to her since then, whether the ball has ever shown her anything useful.

But I've spent too much of today talking to people.

Mom phoned a little while ago because Marc's away at a conference and she wanted to know how we're doing. And then she began to go on about how wonderful the Pope had been in Toronto, how brave he'd been considering his terrible health, and how inspiring it was to see so many young people turn out to see him. They were absolutely ecstatic to see him, you could just tell. Mom isn't a Catholic. In fact, her own Pentecostal mother believed that Catholics belonged to the devil's company. Grandma's no longer alive, but she once held me and whispered about the demons that infest a room waiting for people to enter it. Mom's not that weird, but she still believes, and I replied that there's too much religion in the world already; the Pope should have stayed home. Normally I wouldn't have said anything, but this afternoon there'd been a girl in the library, a faultless seven years old, and her twisted parents had seen fit to dress her in a T-shirt showing some big pink Band-Aids above which were the words "Mommy uses these." On the back of the T-shirt was the message "God used these," and there they were, the colour of bronze, no-nonsense spikes, long and sharp, ready for flesh.

Mom and I have already had our scraps about religion but she won't let it go. Not that she tries to convert me; it's just that she can't imagine a world without God. So I said a few things.

But as she said goodbye tonight, Mom told me that she'd pray for Rory, who was behind a closed door in her room in front of her computer. I thanked her, but kept this information to myself. Rory, Rory, Rory—everyone used to say as they blew wet bubble kisses on her fat white tummy. Rory, short for Aurora, the first grandchild on both sides, Rory my daughter, who still sleeps on Barbie sheets, Rory my anorexic daughter who resists her life, says no to the world by starving herself.

Someone who didn't know me might think I'd keep a close eye on what chat rooms Rory visits when she's alone with a computer. Everything's on the Net. I've visited sites where fellow anorexics can trade tips on how to beat the doctors, keep parents off their backs. But you have to be very, very careful. If I censor Rory, she'll immediately see me as her enemy. And that's the last thing she needs. I know this because I too was an anorexic, and I know that that particular brand of misery is one that literally swallows you whole. Even if I put my foot down harder than I do, Rory would ignore me. I haven't searched on the Net for sites that help the parents of anorexics; I understand the disease from within. Other people—when you're anorexic—they're not even a blur. Every moment of day or dream has one aim: to battle fat. Nothing else exists. I still mentally identify the exact number of calories of whatever I eat. I'm not going to monitor Rory; let her surf. She and I are involved in a war that's all the more terrifying because it's so complicated.

I was angry when I was anorexic, and I'm angry again, but it's a different kind of anger. This isn't how I'd planned on spending my forties.

It was my neighbour Donna who warned me about subversive web sites. We sat outside on the patio for an hour or so just before dinner tonight. That is, until I'd said something wrong and she'd slammed her can of non-alcoholic beer down on the side table. Donna apologized, and so did I, but I told her I had a headache and after she left I hosed away the mess. I've often tried to look at life through Donna's eyes, but I can only get so far and then I have to stop—there's some kind of lunacy there.

According to my husband's sign at the costume party so long ago, he'd been guilty of poisoning the fruit belonging to someone's sacred animal. Which is absurd because Marc loves animals. Becoming a veterinarian was probably his calling, but he strayed into other work. Though it's probably because of Marc that I notice the non-human world as it happens around me. I'm probably better at life than he is, but neither of us is that happy being around most people.

When Donna was talking, a caterpillar began walking around the edge of one of the buckets I leave outside to catch the rain. Wandering around the bucket's lip, it would lift itself up and seek out something solid to hold, find only air, and then fold down to the green rim and start walking all over again. It must have made at least twenty trips before I flipped it onto the grass. The caterpillar was the second insect I've looked at today. The first was a grasshopper floating in the fountain outside the library where I sometimes work. They'd turned the fountain off for maintenance, so the water was utterly flat, shining, and the grasshopper just hung there, half of its body submerged in soft, cruel, wet light. Three of us, women pausing during another day, were soaking our feet. Suddenly the dead grasshopper moved toward the one who'd been wearing clogs and she kicked her feet like a toddler to make it go away.

Donna hadn't noticed the caterpillar on the rain bucket, so I explained what I'd seen, and then told her that my mother would try to find a moral in the caterpillar's journey. I can think of one, I told Donna. It's simple: you might die if you can't conceptualize something as basic as a circle. Or, let's go even further and say that the moral might be: *pay attention when you stumble up against things repeating themselves.*

She looked at me, lit a cigarette, her first that day she said, and got back on track. Without my approval, Donna had been doing research about anorexia for me because she loves to take on a cause. Not only did she print off the information offered on half a dozen web sites, she'd also gotten the phone number of a local group for parents of anorexic children. The meetings are Thursday nights at eight. She volunteered to stay with Rory if Marc and I wanted to go. And we should go, she said. When she found out that Rory was in her room, she told me that if it were her daughter, she wouldn't leave her alone with a computer.

Donna's pregnant, hence the fake beer. And she's terribly ashamed about smoking, but she's also lying. I saw her having her first smoke of the day around seven o'clock this morning. Donna's generosity is genuine enough, I think, but when I told her that Rory wasn't her daughter, that she didn't in fact know what it was like to have children yet, I caught the jaguar that hides behind her eyes.

When we first became neighbours, I'd accidentally hit on some sore spot, or innocently trip over one of her several private hobbyhorses, and she'd rip from zero to one hundred in a split second. Since then, I've learned what to avoid, but sometimes I purposefully get her to blaze when she deserves it. People have their moments, certainly, but I've never met anyone who is as rabid for approval as Donna is. And she's unblinking in her world of certainties.

She changed subjects and asked me what I'd like to contribute to our street party in two weeks. Before I could answer, she said that we could use some chicken wings. And could I bring a bottle of wine, she asked, adding that she knew she could trust my taste—how did she put it? You're someone who knows the difference between a Cab and a Merlot, she'd said, which is true I suppose, but utterly meaningless.

Donna's the soul of the neighbourhood. She's got us all on an e-mail newsletter: from her we learn how to avoid break-ins; from her we hear that the Belinskis' daughter visited from Saskatoon. Local girls can advertise for babysitting jobs on our web site. People can trade their useless items with each other for free. Our street is the envy of the whole city, we learn from Donna.

I'm not much of a joiner I told her.

—It would be good for Rory to come to the party.

—She despises being around people.

—Community is important, you of all people should know that, Donna told me and I'm not succeeding in telling the truth about her. From what I've said, she must sound like a fool, which she isn't by a long shot. She's got a graduate degree in social work, a good and useful job in an office downtown, and a heart that desperately needs to save other people.

And I know how much she wants this baby.

I grew up with controlling people I told her, trying to sound patient, but there was this nasty spin gathering in my voice. Back home when people talked about the importance of the community they really meant: *be like us, please be like us, be exactly like us damn you.*

It's a form of tyranny, I told Donna, which isn't true in every case, but often enough.

At this the jaguar came into her eyes. And it wanted blood. It's unnerving and fascinating to watch. If Donna has a jungle predator inside her, I see myself as a cobra who comes out of a jar and wears a beautiful smile. I offer a truly beautiful smile, my lips a perfect pink kiss, say what I need to say, the smile more important than the words, and then I retreat back inside.

In her fury, Donna becomes one of God's holy angels ready to do battle, except they're her battles, not God's.

—So let me get this straight: you're saying that having a barbecue on our street, getting people out of their houses and talking to each other is a bad thing?

—Why does this matter to you so much?

—Organizing a bike parade is tantamount to being a Nazi?

—Donna, why does this matter to you so much?

Slammed and then foaming beer can, mutual apologies, and a garden hose. Marc had asked me to clean and fill the birdbath each day, but I'd forgotten about it. It was dry, so I hosed it down. Now his birds can drink. And then from over the white wooden fence and shrubbery, the drifting sweetish tang of burning tobacco.

I'm surrounded by people whose lives are spent avoiding reality.

When Curtis, the fellow who cuts our lawn, came by Tuesday, he wanted to know if he'd done a good job on the weeds. Perfect, I assured him, but honestly, who cares? It's just a lawn. He's a decent man, but standing there folding the cheque I'd given him to put into his plaid shirt pocket, he was easily eleven years old, desperate for an adult's approval. The need in his voice was palpable. I can't understand him. He has his own children, and he's in his early thirties—yet he urgently craves compliments about the particular weed killer he uses to destroy dandelions.

Even Marc has difficulty making sense of what's actually happening.

At dinner the night before he left for his conference, he praised Rory for eating her food, and then he went on about how he'd like to buy her a present. He'd seen a girl walking down the street with her pet rat. Now don't laugh, he'd said, though no one was laughing. Or about to. This rat was obviously in love with her, and you could see its energy and intelligence. Now granted, he'd said, the girl had pink hair and you, Ror, don't have pink hair, at least not yet, but she was your age and I was thinking how much you might enjoy having a pet to take care of; the pet store has some rats, and they're really beautiful creatures, very easy to tame the fellow who runs the place said. It would be fun. At his offer to pick one up when he returned from his conference, Rory said she didn't want a pet. Well, you could put it on a diet, Marc offered. I laughed, and even Rory suppressed a smile, but then she asked to be excused from the table. After she'd left Marc turned to me, rolled his eyes, and repeated his wonderful idea. Marc's not stupid; it's just that he can't fathom the problem we have.

Being a parent means that nightmares can strike at any moment. As soon as your child's born, you foresee an entire life of potential dangers. What if she drinks and drives? What if one day she falls for someone who will hit her? What if? The question gnaws at you from the inside out. When Rory was younger and would leave her dolls lying around, their crumpled bodies would become hers, having fallen down the stairs. Ask anyone who has children—this is normal. Having children ruthlessly weds you to life. But I hadn't anticipated that Rory would fall into the same trap I did. She's always seemed so different from me.

When I was fifteen and it had become apparent that my breasts didn't meet anybody's approval, I supposed that if I lost some weight I'd be able at least to have the right figure. I had good legs. If my waist would get narrower, I'd have the necessary curves. At first it was merely a matter of becoming disciplined and getting regular exercise, but one morning my brother changed my life.

I was making my lunch to take to the pool. I taught swimming to kids, really young kids, which was hard work, both physically and mentally. I'd made myself two sandwiches, like I always did, and my brother remarked that if I kept eating like that I would soon be as big as a horse.

I'm sure he didn't mean anything; he was my brother, so how could he? He was only teasing. But that was it. Lunch would be a Diet Coke and carrot sticks. Later, black coffee and cigarettes did just fine. Two years passed that I've never been able to explain to Marc. I'd slipped into a self that had been waiting, patiently waiting for me to find her.

In my entire life, I've never experienced the sensation of raw pride more powerfully than the moment when, as a sixteen-year-old skeleton, I looked over my shoulder one night into the mirror and saw my vertebrae stand out individually and sharp—but the bruises were even better. You should have seen the bruises. My ass and lower back was one long, purple and yellow stain. There was almost no fat anywhere.

But people kept intruding on my life.

I'd always hated showering with other girls, but I soon had to quit teaching swimming because of what other people said when they saw me. The kids in my swimming class pretended I was a monster. Eventually my parents became concerned. People didn't know much about anorexia then and so I was tested for cancer, sent to psychiatrists, had dozens of blood tests. Of course, I stopped menstruating. I was always cold. Eventually a fine grey down covered my body.

But nothing mattered; I pushed further and further, month into month, and then just as suddenly as when I first decided to slice up those carrot sticks, I realized that I was dying. It was in the middle of one night when this bizarre fact came from out of nowhere. It was like I'd found myself on a completely abandoned road in the country, a gravel road; it was absolutely dark, but there wasn't any sky and nothing beside the road either, just me and the narrowness underneath my feet.

And I knew I had to decide.

It took a few days of trying to judge whether I should give a damn one way or the other, and then I settled on keeping my life by returning to it. It was that brutally simple, and I can't make this decision for Rory.

We've talked curled up together on the couch in the living room; we've talked with me screaming at her while she's been lying in her bed and she's pulled up the sheets over her head. "Eyes and ears," I've ordered, a phrase that I first learned to use when she was a child. I want your eyes and ears; you must give me your attention when I talk to you. I've let her know that I know exactly, precisely, what she's going through. I know every moment, every strategy and calculation to deceive. I was good, very, very good at hiding my lust for starvation. I've wished that I'd kept a diary as a teenager so I could show it to her because she can't accept that she's anyone but herself, and she doesn't have any disease, she says. I've told her that her body is soon going to start eating itself. The important organs first.

I've told her that there's nothing she has to live up to, and that one day she'll understand that no one's ever really watching as you live your life. She just looks at me, and refuses to speak. Nothing I say is real to her. I've told her that the happiest moment of my life was her birth, that she owes it to herself to one day have a baby. I've abandoned her in the psych ward for a weekend.

Tonight I could feel her resenting me as we sat at the kitchen table, both of us eating, then sitting over tea for the mandatory twenty minutes so she can't keep food in her mouth and spit it out. She's always hated throwing up, so I know she's not bulimic. While I was loading the dishwasher, I accidentally cut myself on the knife I'd used to make chicken salad, comfort food for both of us. I asked her to get me a Band-Aid as I rinsed my hand under cold water.

"Did you ever cut yourself, Mom?" she asked.

"When I was sick you mean?"

Because Rory won't admit that she's sick she ignored me, and went to get the Band-Aid for my finger.

"I'm doing what I want to do."

"You're too young to know what you want," I replied.

I knew it was a mistake to say this as soon as the words came out of my mouth, and I tried to lessen their force by telling Rory that almost no one understood themselves in any way that was useful. But the damage was done. She kept opening and closing her fists.

I managed to convince her to watch a movie with me, and then Mom phoned and Rory quickly escaped into her room. And now she's asleep, and Marc's called. He's been away for two days now. It's only been two days, and I could hear the relief in his voice. Finally he's gotten away from us, his two troubled women.

Bring some wine home from the States I told him, filling him in about Donna's street party.

The conference is boring, no surprise, but New Orleans is wonderful he'd said; you'd love it. It works twenty-four hours a day trying to convince you that your life has been bereft of sloppy sex. The air's too wet to breathe. The streets are unashamedly dirty; it's like the whole city's a huge and intricate music box that's crammed with all manner of excess. If only we could move, he said. Everybody here's a performer. You'd love it, he said again.

Last night on Bourbon Street, he told me, there'd been a vampire. For five bucks you could take his picture, and he was drinking some wine, a genuine import from Romania called Vampire. Blood drips down the label. It's not very good, he'd said, but Donna will flip. I'll buy her a bottle; it'll be a present that heals the rift between you. I found this necklace with alligator heads for Rory. She'll love it. You'll never guess what I've got for you. They're alive and perfect, he told me. Getting them back across the border won't be a problem. And, Marc said, *and* I bought us some good luck voodoo dolls. One for each of us.

Oh, here's a story for you, Marc said. Howard, this guy I met at the banquet tonight just got hustled. He's only just left my room because he had to have a drink. After dinner, he'd gone out for a walk. He'd been on Canal Street, that's the main street, it goes down to the river; it's filled with camera shops oddly enough, and anyway, these two kids come up to him, ask him if he wants his shoes shined and, before he can say anything, they wipe his feet with a rag. But he wasn't wearing shoes; he'd had on sandals. And then they want twenty bucks. So, he gives them what they want. I mean, the street's always busy; he could have just walked away. He's one embarrassed fellow, but I told him he shouldn't worry about it. After all, he doesn't have to tell anyone.

When Marc asked to speak to Rory, I told him that she'd gone to bed early.

—How is she?

—Angry. And she's talking about knives. She asked me whether I'd ever cut myself when I was anorexic.

I could hear him swallow some wine as he took this new information in.

—Oh Christ. I can't stand this. Is she safe?

—Well, she's probably dreaming. No telling what that means. But I'm here, Marc. She's safe.

—Is that supposed to mean that I'm not there for her?

—No, Marc. You had to go to the conference. You needed a break.

—Attending motivational seminars isn't exactly a vacation.

—I know.

—I hate this job. I want to buy a rat. Just for me. I had my cards read today.

—And?

—She said I should write a letter to someone I love. So after Howard left, I pulled the desk away from the wall, sat on the floor and wrote your name on the back of the desk. I circled your name in a cartoon bubble and had it coming out of the mouth of a hooded lizard.

—I wish I could be there with you.

—Moi aussi.

But it didn't last, this relief my husband had found in New Orleans, because his voice began to crumble as we spoke again about Rory, and there's nothing either of us can do.

I wish there were, but there aren't any distractions from this disease.

And now this house I find hard to love anymore has been dark for hours. I've checked in on Rory, as I've always done, and she's lost to sleep, her ugly and precious arms curled over her head, the way she's done since she was a baby. You can't imagine, I whispered to her as she slept, you can't even slightly imagine how different everything will all become.

And I believe this. Everything utterly changes. I swear I know this to be true. But there are still other things, incomprehensible things that I've kept from her, my daughter, my suffering daughter who doesn't know how to stop being alone.

Writing Letters to Those You Love

— That morning in the waiting room, a man Eric had never seen before asked him at least a dozen times if he didn't think things were happening too fast. People go too fast, nobody knows anything but go, go, go, he'd said, taking in the tiny room, tidying his jacket, then starting up all over again. Eric gave him a cigarette to get rid of him, knowing he'd have to smoke it outside. On a table lay magazines, old news he'd forgotten, a brochure sporting a baby who needed his parents' immediate investment to go one day to university. Eventually their psychiatrist came down the hallway—cowboy boots, unshaven, drinking Orange Crush, frayed black jeans, eyes looking as if they'd been photocopied. Just after six and every morning he meets people with Orange Crush, thought Eric with admiration. Then, safely inside his office, long before his receptionist arrives, the Kleenex box handy on the round coffee table, he'll ask everyone the same question with his ruined smile.

When it was his turn, Eric said that, apart from the usual things, his mind had started playing tricks on him. At the mall, he'd recently seen a sign advertising "Effective Executions." The Body Shop turned into The Bloody Shop; the word "garage" had become carnage. Then everything would swirl back to what it was supposed to be. This must have been a new one because his doctor nodded his head, smiled, made a note, but said nothing. Behind him was a painting showing a lobster resting on a sheet draped lazily over a chair. Part of me lives in a desert, Eric said. Even though the lobster was bright red, it exuded—Eric thought exhumed—contentment, even confidence. Pictures that I can't account for flash across my brain.

They spoke about these images, his medications were increased, and some lithium was added, the next appointment made, and one of the new patients cast down her eyes as Eric left the waiting room. His pockets were crammed with little boxes, drug samples for which he was bitterly grateful. Eric's health benefits had disappeared a long time ago. Because it was an early morning in August, because the music in the elevator touched the right nerve, he decided to walk awhile before taking the subway home.

Recently married, Eric confusedly loves his tall, marigold wife. She's fond of detective novels, those of P.D. James especially, wishes they could go out more often. They want children but can't afford them. Their school and credit card debts are unbelievable, and rent is sometimes borrowed from his parents. He works sporadically in customer service, soothing irate clients on the telephone for a publishing company that sells financial advice. The management believed his degree qualified him to proofread secretarial letters before they went off in the mail. He and Carolyn talk about going on a vacation someday, perhaps somewhere in the States. California, maybe Oregon. They agree that there would have to be a rocky beach that collects small, finely coloured crabs in pools when the tide leaves, pelicans flying in Vs barely above the waves, fast-tumbling mystical clouds, and windy seclusion.

Eric's been diagnosed with moderate, though worsening, clinical depression. This gives him obsessions, exhaustion, occasional insomnia, torpedoes his memory, sabotages his vocabulary, and slurs his speech. He has a thin skin for some things, fury coming easily and unannounced. Most days, though, an impenetrable, sticky fog simply closes in and interrupts the world again. He has metaphysical clarity and terrible detachment. Things glare. His mind sometimes plays emotional chess against him; it can be a meticulous, hyperbolic, often belligerent adversary. When the D as he calls it, is at its worse, he occasionally gives in and curls up on the floor, and then he rocks and rocks, back and forth, because this thing will never go away. The drugs give him nausea, a transient libido, welcome, sparse recognitions of a self the disease has obliterated, anxiety. He suspects he will die soon.

When Eric first started seeing his psychiatrist, the man had told him that it would take some time to find the right combination of anti-depressants—and they would help him a great deal—but Eric would also need to work hard to push beyond solipsism, recognize that gloom wasn't the entire story. Depression paralyzes thought, his psychiatrist keeps telling him. You need to become more aware of both yourself and the outside world. Recognize that, even though there are a million people in this city, you're not accountable for any of them. Except your wife. Concentrate on her. She's your lifeline. I've treated hundreds of people like you, and almost all of them eventually go on to live better lives.

Eric respects his psychiatrist; he's always admired people whose intelligence was clearly above his. And yet the man didn't understand depression from the inside. His advice to take more interest in the world was off the mark. The world never goes away. It confirms his fears. And worse, Eric can't always distinguish between the outside world and what's happening inside him.

When he goes to the park near their apartment, he sees an ancient lady walking her two dogs, one a young, impatient, greyhound, the other the kind William Wegman dresses up and photographs. This particular dog is missing a front leg. He can get along well enough, but Eric wonders about the missing limb. Was she the sort who'd wanted to bury it or did her vet just throw it out? Is cremation best? Eric often finds the leg in dreams, and gives it back to the dog, who then proudly carries it in his mouth as he strolls through the park. A framed photo of the lady with her dogs would look good at his desk at work, but since they never put him in the same place for his shift, he'd have to carry it with him whenever he was called in. This isn't something he'd feel happy about.

Not wanting to get home before Carolyn left for the office, and feeling thirsty, Eric headed for a coffee and doughnut shop. He liked to sit while and take in the numerous others who weren't off to work that morning either. Out of nowhere, a man, a surprisingly well-dressed man, rushed out in front of him and flew across the street.

Wearing sunglasses, he carried a clarinet trailing a dirty, striped green and white ribbon. Two others now followed, pursuing him into the summer's humidity. The day's pollution was beginning to set in. The sun was still low in the sky, orange, not yet the afternoon's blank boiling white. Shouting out first in rage, then bewilderment, these other men suddenly found themselves reeling, as if they'd been caught in a mirage. The man with the clarinet screamed sonofabitch, cocksuckers over and over. Turning to face his foes, glancing up and down, approving of his new patent leather shoes shining next to the curb, he lifted the clarinet to his lips and savagely began to play.

No one recognized the music he'd chosen to fling back across the street. There were only a few people watching, but none was oblivious. Everything, down to the abandoned mirrors of storefronts, the few parked cars, the newspaper boxes illegible with graffiti, everything shimmered with his anger. Then the man disappeared, his music making way for the gulls overhead. A heart had been scrawled into the sidewalk, and in the spirit of romance, Eric decided to have breakfast with his wife. He bought her a chocolate chip muffin, one of her favourite snacks, himself a cup of coffee for the subway.

When he'd return from an appointment, Carolyn always asked about the session. He didn't blame her, but he felt annoyed just the same, feeling that his privacy was under attack. But he knows he loves Carolyn, the cassette tape he made when the doctor had injected him with sodium pentothal proved that. Eric remembered very little of the experience, and he'd made the mistake of listening to the tape. The drug had softened his voice, making it simultaneously gentle and detached. Before his psychiatrist had fitted the IV tube into a vein on his hand, Eric had been frightened of what the drug would make him reveal. It should have reassured Carolyn that the voice on the tape expressed love for her, but she was horrified by its claim that there was nothing Eric wanted more than to be alone. Carolyn phoned Eric's doctor and he settled her down, telling her that all depressives crave solitude, but Eric also knew how much he needed her.

After his walk, the subway was an immense, busy, terrible, and grimy place, a dreamy, streaked aquarium in the morning rush. People were wet with sweat, one or two delicious perfumes. It was too early for kids, so the train was largely silent. For a moment Eric was pleased to let everyone go off to work, but then he felt afraid he'd never find a real job. Guilt arrived next. The subway doors had closed on Pachelbel's *Canon in D*. Women this summer were carefully painting their toenails dark, metallic blue, shiny grey, cherry black. Could this woman standing in front of him feel his admiration, sense the visions rolling in his head? The classical trio had filled the station with a thick, wonderfully amber sound, making Eric wish that the train would be delayed so he could listen longer.

With closed eyes, he'd watched someone from behind surveying a drenched, green hill. He'd read somewhere that music could make people brave. Shifting his weight as the train pulled ahead into the next station, he heard a voice coming down the aisle asking for money.

At Eric's neighbourhood stop, he often met a street musician, whom, oddly enough, he'd known in high school back in Kingston. Eric had almost forgotten him. The guitarist had dropped out of school early, turning up at parties now and then, usually with grass, which gave him a half-hour of popularity. The slow tumble from his teens into the sharply unfamiliar world of begging must have been imperceptible. Would the smoothly worn songs of Cat Stevens and Neil Young—allowing him a busker's license with the transit authorities—even feel the same now? Eric had spoken with him the first time he'd seen him, and couldn't decide whether offering some change would be offensive or not. He's tried to avoid him since.

Eric wasn't aware that he was wearing what Carolyn called his "ugly face," something she'd grown to fear. It showed a burning detachment. She doesn't entirely understand that the urgency in Eric's life is that he's trying to avoid suicide. Of course he hasn't told her how frequently the word pops unannounced into his brain.

Carolyn's told him that when she looks at him she sometimes

doesn't see anyone she knows. Eric doesn't want to hurt his wife and because his psychiatrist had said that it would be useful for him to recognize that his problems didn't dominate the world, Eric forced himself to look at the other people in the subway.

Seated beside him, a Sikh read an old Stephen King novel. Its cover showed a pair of handcuffs affixed to an old fashioned brass bed, the presumably soiled sheets lovingly disordered by the paperback's designer. Across the aisle, an elderly man with a pink and grey gym bag fastened together with safety pins, neatly folded his hands together in greeting and said, "Good Morning, Gentlemen" in a strange way. Despite the other's attempt to keep reading, the old man persisted in talking about the morning, opening up the gym bag and pulling out a small photo album. There were colour aerial photographs of buildings that looked to be in either India or Russia.

"Amritsar," he beamed, "I was there in '58."

With a visionary tremor in his voice, the man spoke of a youthful job, how he'd been on two-hundred-and-sixteen different types of aircraft, the five-hundred-and-sixty-three thousand miles he'd logged, the forty countries visited. Eric wondered why he was carrying these snapshots with him. Did he spend his days lying in wait for East Indians and Lord knows who else so he might then spring his cache of memorabilia? His face resembled one of those RAF Spitfire pilots in old World War II movies—clipped, lean mustache, high cheekbones, and eyes luminescent—except that now it lived abandoned beneath wildly dirty hair.

As the man jabbered on, a woman stared in Eric's direction, having recognized his specific smell, trying to detect the malignancy in their midst.

A woman not far from Eric told a man that she'd heard him getting some vodka from the fridge. He went on to deny it, saying that he'd only been pouring some orange juice. "I heard the clink of the bottle," she'd countered.

"And the best thing was," the old man said, snapping his fingers theatrically above his face and beaming, "I was paid for it."

"Oh, I've talked with you before," said the Sikh.

Bathurst Station was announced, and the world traveller scrutinized his chequered trousers, gripped his gym bag, and went off to his job at the Exhibition, where he was part of a team that sold refreshments—candy floss, pop, french fries, lots of hot dogs. As the train pulled out of the station, and people jostled for seats, a woman's artificial fingernail abruptly moved in front of Eric—long, for the most part elegantly green, a dull emerald neatly setting off a black and white circle. Yin. Yang. Eric thought of David Carradine. At the fingernail's tip, a tiny gold ring. He could just hear REM from her Walkman.

That morning, music seemed to be everywhere.

The apartment the Clements rent is two floors above a sidewalk where this man sits pretty well every morning selling poetry. His socks are thin, rolled tightly above his ankles as if held together by rubber rings. His poems are both true and ironic, he boasts. He has a different poem each day. Eric's also seen him lined up at the beer store; he prefers large cans of Foster's lager. Quite some time ago, in a moment of what he now believes was lunatic curiosity, Eric asked him whether he would like to come upstairs for a beer. "I have some Foster's," he'd said, and to Eric's dismay, the poet did, in fact, follow him up the stairs.

They sat in the kitchen, a stack of handwritten poems between them, drinking beer, discussing life's up and downs, the cost of photocopying. During lulls in the conversation, the man examined the room, commenting that he too, liked red cupboards, yellow draining boards, Palmolive detergent.

Finally, the poet proclaimed: "Shit man, I tell you, baseball is everywhere."

But then he'd spent some time in the bathroom, emerging with a full make-over, having discovered Carolyn's beauty supplies. Eric had thrown everything out afterward, but what still infuriated his wife was that this man would ring the apartment's doorbell, wait for someone to descend two flights of stairs, and then demand to see her husband. Once during the past winter, he'd violently accused her of keeping all the warm inside, and the police had to be called to get rid of him. When he sees the man, Eric has found it's best to say that he can't read poetry anymore.

When he got home, Carolyn had unfortunately already left for work. The chocolate chip muffin would last until breakfast tomorrow. For the last several months, Eric has been a handyman of the absurd. What he's done, after taking the subway home, is follow a gesture, albeit a gentle one. Eric read the note that Carolyn had left, changed his shirt, made a second pot of coffee, and then turned on his old computer, and returned to his letter to Samantha, a woman he once loved. Writing letters to those you love makes perfect sense, but Eric's been working on this letter in fits and starts for a long time. The letter's an argument, a diary of sorts, and a solitary interrogation—because Samantha locked herself in a car in a garage several years ago, after having turned on the ignition and then waiting for sleep to come.

Eric now thinks he knows what was going through her mind during that time; she would have been remembering things, remembering everything, but without perspective. Eric had been living in another city when he got the phone call a few days later. He's since then reconstructed both of their days—hers, his. It had been a Friday in the late fall. He and Carolyn, not knowing anything at the time, had visited Carolyn's parents for the weekend. He can remember driving north of the city; the sky had been an immense, fierce blue. When he now thinks of Samantha, sometimes Eric can only manage to ask stupid questions—did she play the car's radio that day or not?

Eric knows that it's pointless to write to a dead person, but in his letter he's been trying to come up with reasons as to why Samantha shouldn't have committed suicide. At least that was the letter's original purpose. But the letter's become less an argument and more a collection of details taken from what Eric's seen. By cramming the letter with perceptions, Eric hopes to offset the ugly silence Samantha has given him. Perhaps the dead are famished for sensation. Perhaps without Eric's letter, Samantha would truly disappear.

Beside the uncurtained window in Eric's apartment, there's an almost white lutino cockatiel holding a piece of cucumber while working on the seeds. Behind him on a plate are a few cherries and grapes he's ignored since earlier this morning. The bed's unmade, the magenta skirt and black stockings Carolyn wore to work yesterday are lying on the floor. The phone rang and once again, soon after Eric answers it, the caller hangs up. When the bird discovers that he's alone, he climbs up the side of the cage using his beak, a tiny grappling hook made of cartilage, and standing on a perch, begins to shriek.

Just before he met his wife, she was living in a basement apartment in North York. A student then, she'd done a double major—French literature and computer science. One night she'd woken to someone tapping on her window. As Carolyn tells it, there, in the middle of winter, was an erect penis. She was mostly steamed because she'd been woken up, but the newspapers had been printing warnings, particularly to women living alone. After that she was flashed several times when she went out jogging and there were phone calls as well.

She's never figured out who the man is, and the police have said that nothing can be done until the man actually tries something. About once a month, Eric picks up the phone and whoever it is that's calling waits for a moment, mumbles Carolyn's name, and then hangs up.

"It was that asshole again," Eric says to Jeremy the bird, who is busy shredding newspaper and chuckling.

One night when he and Samantha were living together, Eric had stood naked with a glass of wine in his hand. He didn't know what he was doing. As he stood, the room spun with the traffic light situated directly below the apartment. Facing him, holding her wine glass,

Samantha had small feet, unpainted toenails. She wanted to find out certain things; she was inspired. Urging him on, then lunging, she wanted to duel. This night was a test. Lying in bed afterwards, the bedding having been shaken over the balcony to get rid of the broken glass, she used a towel to staunch the wound on her hand.

Earlier that day Eric held her around the waist while they walked through a park. It was raining, the park was abandoned, and he abruptly folded her down onto the grass, lifted her top and began to kiss her breasts. Then, taking their umbrella, he waded out into the pond, pretending he was an old man. Turning around, he asked: "Do you know who I am?"

"W.C. Fields once said that death would be like a man arriving in the rain, wearing a suit and carrying an umbrella," he tells her.

"You're not wearing a tie."

Later, dripping wet, they entered an elevator to an apartment they'd been subletting. Another woman got on, carrying a basket of laundry. Eric removed his glasses and asked if he could use one of her sheets to dry them. "At one point my great-grandfather spent time on the *Titanic*," he joked, but she said no, he couldn't use her linen, then glanced at the button that showed the floor he lived on.

Trying to get warm in the shower, rinsing shampoo from her hair, Eric asked Samantha if she knew why he had done what he did. "You know how the mind works," he explained, "it needs disturbance, otherwise it forgets everything. I wanted you to remember today."

"We're home now," she said, almost inaudibly, "don't be so sentimental."

"So what do you want Jer?" Eric asks. Another bird begins to sing, a zebra finch, and the cockatiel looks up. Eric loves birds and he has four of them: Jeremy, two finches who are mates, and a new lori who's still hesitant about the salads that are made for them each morning. Eric doesn't know what kind of information Samantha needs to hear so he includes the birds in his letter; details are important. He mentions that early the other morning he'd gotten up to go to work, and Carolyn told him not to worry about the birds, she'd look after them, and he'd hurled *Why can't you get off of my back for once?* into her startled face, the poison already running through his brain. A streetcar goes by, the sun's terribly hot, and he goes to the back porch to have a cigarette, smoke being harmful to the birds. A jet has just gone by, its contrail twisting into a helix and he thinks briefly about cancer. The phone rings again.

"Hello Sweet," Carolyn says, "enjoying your day at home?"

Feeling guilty that he's been writing a love letter to Samantha, rather than Carolyn, Eric tried to put a bounce in his voice.

"It's been great."

"What are you doing?"

"Oh, mostly nothing, Went to see some movies, then Jeremy crapped on my shirt and I'm very seriously thinking about doing some laundry."

This is becoming a refrain, a marital litany which, when translated, means that Eric's feeling guilty that he's at home while his wife's at work.

"Sounds like a great day. Did you get my note?"

"Uh huh."

"I'm so happy Jill's coming over for dinner tonight. We haven't seen her for ages. Have you taken the meat from the freezer?"

"It's marinating in a heap of clam juice, *vin ordinaire* and mustard, several pinches of paprika."

"My husband, the ever-splendid cook."

"Flattery is everything, Carolyn. But I've got to go, Jeremy's screaming to beat the band."

"I can hear him," she says, "aren't we busy!"

"I've got high hopes."

Leaning against the railing of the porch overlooking the alley out back, he notices one of his neighbours arranging some English ivy around the neck of a wooden horse, a horse that was once part of a fair-ground carousel. Her deck is dwarfed by plants and several statues: a swan, some turtles, even a little boy that looks as though he should be pissing into a fountain somewhere in Germany. Tracing out perimeters of the deck is a string of plastic owls and Christmas tree lights. At night, the back of her apartment looks like a beer commercial. She turns around, and looks at him through sunglasses. She's closer to thirty than forty. Because of her white bikini, Eric is embarrassed that she's seen him looking at her.

He likes Jill, an old university friend of Carolyn's, and he knows that his wife loves to have company, but he doesn't want to see anyone tonight, Jill or no Jill. Maybe she'll cancel. Sometimes it's as though the entire universe conspires to keep people from being alone.

And what if cities are moments of copulation? Eric writes, back inside again, continuing his long letter to Samantha, Samantha who never sleeps. *Adam questioning his second wife on the ballooning contagion of virgin births, the abattoir of closely scrutinized jazz. General Motors as monolithic theatre, despite limos and bushels of cops in drag, the hollowing out of voyeurism, Karl Marx, that yucca. People shouting wake me up in the middle of the night Sam,* Eric writes, *and they shout: "God, motherfuck, PARALLELOGRAM!" Satan, the devil in the deep blue sea, patiently dreaming of his return. Doh, a deer, ray, a drop of golden sun, and the comfort of people finally coming home from work, Mozart writing his* Requiem, *a long and boisterous letter to his dead dad.*

Talk with me this once, Sam, now.

But instead of hearing from Sam, Eric recalls an elderly man from earlier that morning. He'd looked as though he'd been born in Eastern Europe, and he was exasperated by something in a poster, stapled to telephone pole. Wearing a dark fedora, he held himself against the pole with one hand. Lifting his aluminum cane, he tried to scrape away the offending paper above him. The telephone pole swarmed with thousands of rusty staples fixed into the wood. The man worked feverishly, responding to an inner necessity, an exacting tribunal that no one else could see.

Thinking about this man, Eric stops typing, leans back, lets his eyes rove around the room, then linger on a geranium. Staring at the plant, he wills it to disappear. A noise from the street startles him, and for an instant he sees the profile of a lizard sunning its flat, green body against a rock. A car has gone by, filling the room with a few notes of music. The fan beside him makes another sweep across the desk, causing a postcard thumb-tacked against the wall to flicker slightly. The moment widens, vanishes, and Eric knows that whatever he writes isn't a map; it can't be used to find anyone. Nothing in his experience has prepared Eric for this kind of life.

No One Can See This

— Walking back from the liquor store, and relieved that it was Friday, Marcie noticed the car with the bumper sticker pass by again. She'd never caught a good look at the driver, but she assumed that he must live in the neighbourhood. Just above the battered car's trailer hitch, a sticker advertised a tattoo parlor. A testimonial from Jeffrey Dahmer guaranteeing that the shop's tattoos were the tastiest, a phone number. The first time Marcie and her boyfriend Ian had become aware of the bumper sticker had been the previous summer when the landlord for the apartment in which they were now living had interviewed them.

Marcie had been surprised when the landlord had informed them that the building was filled mostly with black people. Some people were prejudiced, he'd replied to her, looking over the letter she'd gotten from Student Aid proving she had a student loan. Even though the makeshift office was in the basement, they soon became aware of unidentifiable odours from upstairs. There'd been a heat wave that week and each of them had been soaked with sweat. Down the hallway, the building's single washer and dryer was already busy.

Because of their clothes, Marcie and Ian could have been a young couple going to church. His fedora on the old desk, the landlord, who must have been in his late sixties, wore striped suspenders, and a tightly buttoned white shirt. He didn't appear to be affected by the heat. All the while he'd spoken in an unfamiliar language to his nephew who was standing behind him. He was there to learn the business, and said little. Arrangements were made to sign the lease at the landlord's house later that week, because he needed his wife's signature on the document.

Ian wanted to photocopy the lease, so he and Marcie crossed

the street to the variety store, made a copy, and bought something to drink. Marcie waited on some bleachers in the community ballpark facing the apartment building across the street. Seagulls fed on some french fries by first base; the sun was so powerfully white it leached the grey from their bodies. Behind her a truck changed gears and she wondered how long it would take until they wouldn't hear the traffic.

No one should have to live amidst the sounds of machinery. Waiting for a bus, they were too depressed to talk much, but then Ian started to laugh.

"Did you see that car?" Ian asked.

"No, but let's walk a bit. I don't feel like getting into a bus. It's too sticky."

Ian told her about the bumper sticker.

"Who's Jeffrey Dahmer?"

"A psycho who was arrested with body parts in his fridge. I think he was killed in prison a few years ago."

"Cute, maybe we should get one."

"First we should get a car."

"No, I was thinking we could put it on our refrigerator."

"That's my Marcie," he laughed. "So what do you think?"

"Oh Ian, it's awful—do you really think we can live here? Are we making a mistake?"

"It won't be so bad."

A middle-aged man in a Speedo bathing suit, mirrored sunglasses, and bright yellow thongs passed by them carrying a towel, a radio, and something in a paper bag. The bathing suit was a Union Jack. The man spat out a sunflower seed.

"Men his age just shouldn't, should they? Remind me when I get older not to inflict myself on the public like that, okay?"

Ian had never before said anything that spoke so strongly of their having a long-term future together.

The following week they'd trekked to the landlord's home, sat on plastic-covered furniture, drank tea, and argued about the rent because the 49 on the lease had been changed, and not very subtly, to an 89. But the photocopy proved that they'd agreed to pay $849, not $889. For some reason the old man kept pointing to his hairy ears as he backed down, saying there must have been a mistake. When they moved in some weeks later, a card was slipped under their door late one evening. Signed by the landlord's wife, it wished them true happiness in their new home. Marcie recalled that the woman had been tall with neat fingernails, unhurried eyes, and no lipstick.

Moving in with Ian was the best thing Marcie had ever done. Starting a new kind of life, it was so easy to be happy.

When she'd first arrived home that Friday afternoon there'd been some cards in the mailbox because it'd been her birthday earlier that week. Marcie's older and much more settled sister Lori wrote that she'd sent some maple leaves last week to her family's new foster child in Ghana. That meant that Lori supported at least three children in the developing world. The bubble envelope Lori had sent Marcie also included some chestnuts, and a birthday cheque. Apparently Lori had been in town shopping for groceries, and thinking about their childhood, had parked her van in front of Yantzi's, though it wasn't Yantzi's anymore, and she'd searched for two perfect glossy-waxy, chestnuts.

Mr. Yantzi had always run his barber's business out of his house. His red and white striped pole was utterly dwarfed beneath the tree that lured kids after school every autumn. They would scour his yard for the biggest chestnuts that would then be threaded with a spike and shoestring. Their lust for chestnuts often turned into vicious fights. For a few days, several patches of grass in the school's playground would become dirt amphitheaters where mostly boys would lay a chestnut down for their opponents to strike. With luck the other player would miss, maybe even smack a stone hidden beneath the dirt.

Beneath Marcie's childhood's sky—a balloon stretched tight, almost bursting—it was lemony green and bright, unnatural shadows.

Theories abounded as to what would make the chestnuts tougher—soak them in water, then put them in the freezer, or better yet, coat the shells with wax from a clear candle. The eight-year-old Marcie had recognized early that magic, not science, worked best. Only those that were the deepest brown and then polished with spit and left to sleep overnight on her bed beneath her ruby red washcloth would become champions, gleefully smashing as many as four or five other chestnuts before being splintered into jagged chunks of white chestnut meat.

Lori wrote that the birthday money wasn't to be spent on booze or used for bills, but especially not bills the letter made clear with an exclamation mark.

How many people could identify Ghana on a map?

Getting her kids to collect some cheerful leaves for someone they'd only seen in pictures was admirable—and no doubt they'd signed his letter, just as they'd put their scrawled names on their Aunt Marcie's card—but what's a little boy somewhere in Africa to do with maple leaves, Marcie wondered. The two sisters went along parallel lines far enough, but Marcie always jogged off into extremities from which Lori recoiled. When they'd been in high school, Lori and Marcie had participated in a Fast For Hunger campaign. Students got pledges for the hours they fasted; they were advised to drink juice and go no longer than two days. Lori stopped when she was supposed to, but Marcie had thought that was too easy. Two days didn't mean anything. She gave in on her fifth day because her mother started talking nonsense about anorexia.

Marcie spent her sister's money on some frozen beef stroganoff and two bottles of wine, one for her that afternoon, the other the Italian kind Ian liked, a big one that would last the entire evening. She'd ask him if he knew where Ghana was when he got back from work.

He wouldn't be able to have a shower because the hot water was off again, the third time that month. Public Health wouldn't do anything unless it was off for three consecutive days. They'd have to heat up pots of water on the stove. After coming home from his part-time roofing job, Ian hated baths because he was so grimy. He'd be upset that he couldn't have a shower, but at least they had the satisfaction that the landlord paid the utilities.

Their apartment was on the third floor, the top of a building that overlooked a severe dip in the road. There was a traffic light at the bottom of the two hills, and at least once a week Marcie would hear screaming tires, a pause of maybe a second, and then the collision. Marcie majored in history at university—she was beginning to learn how many deaths occurred over the centuries because of geography bizarrely connecting with human laws.

In July, the temperature often rose above forty degrees in the apartment. During those nights whose slow, jangled hours wore the many kinds of light that passed outside the windows, Marcie and Ian would wake up sporadically and make their way to the fridge to stand naked in front of the open door and swig down Gatorade, a moment of cool air on their skin before they collapsed face down on the sheets once more. In all the seasons, the walls, cupboards, kitchen floor, and even the bathroom mirror sweated cockroaches.

The night they'd moved in, the guy who was moving out had slammed his fist down on the top of the fridge to kill a cockroach before he and his buddy removed the last of his Victorian furniture. Marcie was sad to see the fancy dresser and desk removed because it had made the apartment look as though it could be lived in with some feeling of grace. Marcie had accustomed herself to battling the tribe of surprisingly canny insects that infested the apartment, eventually discovering the best brand of traps, though her mind would gag for the rest of her life when it recalled the disinfectant the landlord sprayed.

The bottle of wine she'd bought for herself to drink that late afternoon had been chosen carefully. It had to be red, cheap, but not garbage either. Marcie curled her bare feet under her on the afghan on the couch, a million colours long, knitted for her by her mother when she still lived at home. The instant her tongue met the wine in the glass her blood began to climb. And the vague anxiety she'd been starting to feel daily immediately began to disappear.

A motorcycle gang had a clubhouse next door. Later, when she tossed the empty bottle into the dumpster before Ian came home, she'd see that one of their guard dogs had a puppy. It pranced around its chained mother, nosed along the packed dirt and autumn leaves behind the wire fence. At the end of the biker's yard a garage sunk unevenly into the soil. The dogs couldn't see the huge skull, surrounded in fire, which had been painted on the wall facing the apartment building.

It was an amazing thing to have your own apartment.

When her mom had first seen Marcie's new home, arriving unannounced and then refusing to accept that her daughter could ever live with a man without marrying him, she'd picked up the yellow pages and booked a cleaning service to do a one-time-only thorough scrubbing of the place. She paid for the cleaning in advance with her credit card. All of this is disgusting she'd said. I don't know what's worse, you or this apartment.

But that Friday afternoon in early October, the bottoms of Marcie's feet held a sheen of dust, insecticide and grease from last night's meal, and she wanted to coast for a few minutes on the wine before picking up a pencil to start researching her history term paper on the organization of ghettos during the Nazi occupation of Poland or Hungary, she hadn't yet decided which. A chestnut fell on the floor from the coffee table.

According to some boys, you could continue the game as long as the slightest piece of chestnut held to its string. Marcie recalled her argument with Ross Gingerich, who'd absurdly claimed that even the wax on his string qualified.

When she protested, he reminded her that she'd been adopted, knowing this would bring tears. But Marcie had been able to find her older sister on the playground and that had been that. It would be just like Lori to send the chestnuts to jog her memory, make her recall that ancient act of sisterly solidarity.

A roach made its way down the wall. Before they'd gotten used to the cockroaches, Ian and Marcie had seriously fantasized about going by the landlord's house at night and dumping a large, open envelope filled with the insects into the mail slot in his front door. But now, they simply kept a box of Kleenex in every room so that upon sighting a roach they could crush it before it got away.

After throwing the squashed insect in the garbage, Marcie placed the wine in the middle of the coffee table her sister had given her a couple of years earlier. It was a hand-me-down; because the table's edges were too sharp for toddlers, Lori had passed it on to her sister. Going over the photocopies she'd made of articles on the Holocaust, Marcie picked up her highlighter so she could better understand what she was reading. She began to pay close attention to the articles that referred to orphaned children.

After classes that morning, she'd worked at the tutoring agency uptown that specialized in students with learning disabilities, but most of them were merely lazy kids who'd been born to wealthy parents. Always polite, they never let her forget that she was the hired help, perhaps necessary, but only for the moment.

There was much better money serving drinks in the strip club a few blocks north of their apartment, but she'd decided to quit that job the morning she'd stepped out of a coffee shop and had seen two of the Asian dancers get into a car with a regular customer. Opening their doors with a flourish, he hadn't seen Marcie, but after he ran his hand over one of the girl's long hair, Marcie caught his red, almost purple, face above the steering wheel as he cut into traffic and surged down the street. Marcie wondered whether the woman who'd been ushered into the back seat of his car was happy that she wasn't the one who had to make conversation in the front.

Choosing a single seat next to the window on the bus that would take her to the subway, Marcie felt lucky to be going to the university library. She hoped the man would be impotent when he got the dancers in bed. It was seeing those women get into the car that had made her decide to quit her job. It would be hard, but she'd find something else. Though she knew she'd never find anything that paid as well as the club. Probably the only person in the city who enjoyed its transit system, Marcie then did what she loved to do—she became invisible by opening her book. But the autumn light was too bright on the page. Marcie began, as she often did, to make up stories about the people she saw on the bus.

Behind her, a teenager who'd vowed to herself that she'd have a boyfriend by Christmas tugged on the cord so she could get off at the next stop with enough time to catch the talk show on TV that really understood where she was coming from. A couple having fertility problems sat at the back of the bus. The man wore a tweed jacket and held a vial of semen under his armpit with one hand, the other nestled in the woman's. After they dropped off their specimen for testing, they were going to treat themselves to a late breakfast. Many of the cars going by had Jamaican flags on either their bumpers or hanging from their rearview mirrors.

And Marcie believes that there's a cry that builds, then breaks from some people, a cry that isn't solely grief, that's so pure and lasts for so long, sometimes stretching over years, that it shakes whoever can sense it.

The hot water in their apartment was back on late Saturday, so Marcie didn't need to boil water for her bath. Some friends were coming over for a dinner party. Living with Ian, Marcie had discovered the delight of trying out recipes. He was cooking sausage soup, made with a dark Belgian beer, and later they'd serve it with red wine and Edam cheese, thick round Italian bread—the kind that gives off a dust of flour.

Marcie's childhood home held four spices: salt, pepper, chili powder, and a steak tenderizer. In small town Ontario, the topic of food dominated most conversations. When she visited her parents, a two-hour bus trip away, they still talked endlessly about their meals.

Retired now, her father fussed over the barbecue. He'd cook steaks for the family and each time proudly declared that they were the best he'd ever tasted. What was it about them and food? It wasn't unusual for one of the neighbours, Dolores, to hold forth on her boys' good appetite. Marcie thought that this obsession with her sons' eating habits would make sense if they'd been children; but in fact, they would soon be leaving high school. And worse, Dolores would be taken seriously.

When people back home weren't eating, or talking about eating, or talking about their cars, they'd fret over flowers they'd planted around garden ornaments—her parents had two Dutch kids kissing on the front lawn, a statue they hid in the garage at night so it wouldn't be stolen. Giant monarch butterflies clung to the white vinyl siding of their house. They scrubbed the birdbath twice a day, experimented with pesticides. All summer, everyone on the whole street was feverish about decorating their various warrens. It seemed to Marcie that the people back home spent their entire lives merely hurrying from one passive sensation to the next.

Ian shouted from the kitchen asking whether Marcie wanted another beer.

"Most definitely," Marcie answered.

Ian brought the beer, and complimented Marcie on how she made the soap bubbles look beautiful.

"Come on in, come on in," Marcie said, "it's a treat to drink a cold beer in a hot bath."

"Are you this friendly with every waiter?"

"Only if he looks like you."

Marcie loved Ian, but she was used to keeping much of her life to herself. No one knew that only the week before Marcie had filled the bathtub with cold water and all the ice cubes she could find in the freezer. She lay in the tub for as long as she could take it because she'd been reading of children standing naked in the snow at Treblinka waiting their turn in the gas chambers.

When she'd met her history professor in his office to discuss her essay, she'd wept, saying she wanted to drop the course but felt that to do so would be somehow immoral. She couldn't understand how he could spend his life researching and teaching the Third Reich. For some reason she trusted this man she hardly knew; but what did he expect her to do with the images and information he'd provided? His course was ruining her other classes. But perhaps that was necessary. She asked him about the framed pastel drawing behind him.

"It's Goethe," he said, and then added, "a German poet."

"How can you have anything German in your office? I mean, aren't you Jewish?"

The professor was used to such talks with distraught students for this course on the Holocaust that he taught every other year. He tried to explain the limits of historical knowledge, and also the importance of demystifying Nazism. The need to correct Hollywood with facts. Students, even men, cried in his office, though he wondered most about those who quit half way through the course, which always started with a full enrollment. Most stayed. Were those students who dropped the course more morally sensitive than the others? Or maybe they were just lazy; he was proud of his reputation as a demanding professor.

It was certainly true that anything to do with Nazism fascinated people. Over the years, numerous students had thought he was a Jew. The first time a student had made this assumption at least a decade ago, he'd almost laughed the thought was so absurd. He didn't look Jewish in the least. The professor was a confident man, but that moment, when he recognized how easily the prejudice had come to him, he felt temporarily stalled.

"But what am I supposed to do?" Marcie asked.

"You can read differing accounts so that your essay is balanced."

"That's not what I mean. My sister supports foster children in poor countries. But you can't send money to a Jewish family in Hungary in the '40s."

"As you know, Marcie, history can't change events. It's hard for historians to respond emotionally. At least in their writing."

"I just don't know what to do. Can I be honest? I was adopted. And I keep wondering about orphaned children during the war— their terrible fear. I see a boy's face looking out of the back of a school bus and it flashes into my head that he could have been someone taken away by the Nazis. I'm sorry but do you have a Kleenex? I can't even look at a bulldozer without thinking about a place like Treblinka."

"You're a decent person Marcie," he offered, "but no one can be rescued from the past." He told her that she could come and see him again, that he respected her, and then suggested some primary material she might look into for her essay. He told her to footnote everything and explained how footnotes could also be used to expand her argument. The key is precision, he advised.

"Anything you want to listen to?" Ian asked as he got out of the bathtub and dried himself.

"Our new Tea Party."

When their guests arrived, Marcie uncharacteristically kissed them on the cheek. Living with Ian made her feel differently about herself, more experimental.

"Oh my," said Katrina, not her given name, but one she'd chosen upon entering her new life in the city and the university.

Ian astonished Marcie by saying that someday she would make someone a beguiling wife.

After the meal, the dinner plates became ashtrays. Katrina mucked around with the orange candles, so wax spread, like dull lava, across the purple tablecloth. Dirty dishes crammed the kitchen counter and sink. Unlike her mothers' dinner guests, Marcie's wouldn't offer to wash dishes. She'd have to clean up before going to bed or the cockroaches would have a feast.

None of Marcie's new friends had ever played chestnuts as kids. Katrina wanted to try a game, but they couldn't find any spikes, only sewing needles to skewer the chestnuts. It so happened that only one of Marcie's guests knew where to find Ghana on a map. Ian opened up all the wine, announcing that no one could leave until every bottle was empty.

Marcie loved it when he got really drunk with her.

He got out the camera, wanting to take experimental pictures. He shot a roll, but the only one that would turn out was of a cockroach coated with the orange wax and placed on Katrina's boyfriend's forehead as he lay on the floor.

Finally, finally, Marcie had found herself at home. Her friends spoke about the things that mattered in a language that she knew well. They lived in the same world she did—a situation she'd never experienced before. For the first time in her life, she didn't have to justify who she was.

They were listening to *Stoned Immaculate*, a tribute CD to the Doors that Jared—someone Marcie had met at the tutoring service—had bought that afternoon after work. Someone who savoured his self-possession, Jared had removed the liner notes from the attaché case he always carried and passed them around.

Headphones hung around his neck from his ever-present Walkman.

The muted television and candles made a bouncy kind of light.

Jared told them about visiting Morrison's grave in Paris and leaving an airplane bottle of scotch at the shrine. Other people had left dope; someone had left her panties. Jared thought Stone Temple Pilots' cover of "Break on Through" was better than any of their own music.

William S. Burroughs spoke from the CD of the Lizard King's drowning death in a bathtub. Marcie surprised Ian by telling everyone that they were saving up for a trip to Europe; they would definitely check out the cemetery in Paris.

Then, on another track, Morrison's all-American voice, gleeful as the darkest fairytale, confided that upon death you would have to watch your whole life as a movie that replayed eternally. So you better make sure that it contained some good scenes, he advised, laughing to the background guitar.

Anton, from Marcie's history class, said they'd better have some more wine, just in case Morrison was right.

They discussed Morrison's theory. They smoked some dope.

Someone noticed that it had become the next day. It was too late to go across the street to the variety store and get some potato chips.

"But there's something wrong," Marcie said, slamming her wine glass on her sister's coffee table. "I mean, it's fine for Jim Morrison to talk about watching your life forever—he had a great life—but what if your life sucked? And what if it wasn't your fault? What if you were some kid killed by the Nazis for Christ's sake?"

"Don't worry about it Marcie," Jared said. "It's just a metaphor. Morrison ripped it off from somebody else." He handed her what was left of a joint after inhaling very, very deeply.

"I don't care, it's just too weird," Marcie said, feeling tears approaching. She opened a beer and went outside and stood on the balcony and took in the street.

Different from Marcie, who made no concessions to her femininity, warm, warm, warm Katrina pictured herself lounging in a huge theatre watching her life-as-eternal-movie and then she decided to undo her emerald velour blouse and show off her latest piercing. A gold hoop threaded her left nipple.

Katrina's boyfriend realized how little he knew about her.

"I don't remember you doing this," he told her.

"So where did you get your work done?" Jared asked.

"Oh, I did it myself," Katrina said.

Ian forgot about his camera because he was gambling whether he could get away with dipping his finger in his wine and painting Katrina's other breast. Marcie was still out on the balcony, and besides, Morrison wouldn't have hesitated.

Someone in the back part of the building ordered a pizza.

The bikers' dogs had been fast asleep, and the lights from a car pulling in to the parking lot woke them up. But they were well trained, and would only bark if someone were stupid enough to climb over the fence.

"Any requests?" Ian asked.

Katrina said that she'd look over their music collection, and she promised to come up with a surprise.

Marcie steadied herself by leaning against the balcony railing. Her sister would be expecting a thank-you letter for the birthday money. She went through what she had to do the next day to see if she could find the time. Sunday was her favourite day and she hoped she'd wake up before Ian so she could go for a walk by herself and laze around in a coffee shop. She'd people-watch, read the newspaper, and then she'd surprise Ian by bringing him a cherry–cheese danish. Then she'd have to get back to her essay.

One of the cars coming down the hill toward her looked exactly like the one that belonged to the man who'd bought the dancers a few weeks ago. It was precisely the right colour. Marcie waited until it got closer, got a good grip on her beer bottle's long neck, and aimed for the windshield. Foam and amber glass erupted on the hood of the car. Marcie ducked behind the curtain by the sliding doors. A man got out of the car and yelled up at the building. He had to wait for traffic to pass until he could cross the street to the telephone booth.

"We have to think fast," Marcie told her guests, "I think we're going to get a visit from the cops."

"Why?" asked Katrina, "we haven't done anything."

Marcie filled them in.

"Oh for Christ's sake, Marcie, why the hell did you do that?" asked Ian.

Katrina said there wasn't any time for arguing. They should stay put. If the police did come and they were outside waiting for a bus, they might ask questions. Then she told Marcie to get into her nightgown. They could all hide in the bedroom.

Jared thought that they should go out back and walk down a few blocks and grab a cab. Besides, how could the cops get into the building? They wouldn't have keys.

"I like Katrina's idea better," Anton said, "let's get some beer and camp out in the bedroom."

They blew out the candles, switched off the television, drunkenly tidied up, turned off the music, and waited in the bedroom.

The light from a cruiser began spinning around the walls, and two police officers slipped into the building alongside the bewildered pizza deliveryman. Eventually they knocked at Marcie and Ian's apartment.

"Someone from this building threw a beer bottle at a car a little while ago. Do you know anything about that?" asked one of the cops.

Marcie claimed she'd been sleeping. She'd woken up when they knocked.

"Are you sure you weren't having a party? Maybe someone did it when you weren't looking. Are there any other people inside?"

"I told you, I was sleeping. There's no one here. I didn't even hear a party."

"Do you usually go to bed this drunk?"

"You can't treat me like this," Marcie said, poison flooding her brain, "I'm not black you know."

The taller cop looked at her with contempt, and advised her to get back to bed, she needed to sleep it off.

Fucking fascists, she said to herself.

Sometime later, Marcie woke up. She couldn't tell if it was the sound of the ambulance outside or because the tidal wave in her dream was about to burst across the apartment building that had awoken her.

In her dream, the park across the street had already been spewed up by the massive wall of water that smashed through the bedroom window. A bridge from her hometown had spun up and wrinkled across a sky that then sprayed water. Subdued now, her fear had torn within her, scrambling in its efforts trying to escape, and she could still see her dream, though it was beginning to fall away.

There was some beer left in the fridge, and the cool concrete on the balcony felt good on her bare feet as she watched the scene below. It didn't look as if anyone was hurt badly.

She'd been sleeping so deeply she hadn't heard the collision.

She didn't really want to be seen looking at the accident, especially if those cops were the same ones who had come earlier, so she went inside and sat back in her swivel chair by her card table desk. She leaned her head back slowly. Even that drunk, and after helping Ian when he threw up in the bathroom after everyone left, she was still in charge. The night could still be hers. She loved the sensation of letting her hair fall back toward the floor. She'd take some aspirin before she went back to bed.

An image suddenly sprang into Marcie's head, flew up and flashed from nowhere. It showed an utterly humiliated man in a comic book saying, "Oh my God, not that joke, not here."

She worked at the memory a bit. It came from a Christian tract made especially for children she'd received at Bible school. Every summer, shortly after school had ended, her mom had always insisted that she and her sister attend vacation Bible school at the Baptist Church. After Bible school, they then had to take swimming lessons.

One summer the kids had been given a black and white cartoon tract.

It was the story of a man who'd had it made with fancy clothes and a sports car, a huge house. A mansion with a strangely shaped swimming pool. Marcie could remember that the cartoon man had large sideburns and wavy black hair. But then he died. And before judgment, God played a movie showing every moment of his life. But the thing was, everyone who'd ever lived was in the audience. First the man would become naked to all history, and then he would find out whether his life meant Heaven or Hell.

She finished her beer, and looked to see if any wine was left. There was. She held her mind tenderly, knowing from experience that if she weren't careful, her brain would threaten to shake itself loose from her skull.

And she became very angry. And she also realized the importance of her future, what she eventually needed to do.

"Bring on the cameras," Marcie whispered, pulling back some more of the dark wine.

"I'm ready for my movie," she said, "I'll show every one of you what's true."

She didn't hear Ian come up behind her.

"Are you okay?" he asked, swaying a little.

And this, too, was exactly what needed to happen.

Fathers, Sons

— There's a moment in the world when a prairie blizzard almost takes itself for granted, the snow at night, no longer furious, only keeps covering and covering. In the city, the dark glows, the streetlights, casting an almost imperceptible pink, are faultless shreds of neon. And the sky pushes itself down so close you could reach up into it and gut it by standing only on a picnic table.

It's hard to ignore books, though sometimes he tries.

Because Jeremy teaches literature for a living, on a night like this one, he can't help but think of Joyce's Gabriel Conroy seeing death in the whirling white. He tells students that writing clarifies thought, and perhaps it does. He keeps a statue of the Venus de Milo handy, the colour of a basement apartment carpet, mottled orange and blackish silver, for when students ask for a definition of the word *kitsch*. On a good day he hopes that the few stories and poems that they read will pour Drano on their sentimentality; on bad days he prepares lectures in the car.

This past summer—his son in the infant seat taking in whatever was outside the window beside him, across that astonishing arc that reaches, second by second, into a baby's consciousness, a pool that still was wordless—this past summer, sand in their shoes, a father with his son driving home from a park that has baby swings, when the radio announces that a local man has died in a go-karting accident. His name is familiar. Reaching over to turn up the radio's volume, Jeremy suspects the man had been in one of his classes, but he can't be sure unless he pulls the name up on a computer screen.

Instead of going home, they go to the university, Jeremy and his son. While Jeremy sits at his desk, his baby grabs a splendidly designed hippo from a large ceramic dish, the dish the work of a friend's wife who gave it to Jeremy on a winter morning in Vancouver. Back then he was neither a father nor a professor; the woman awkwardly pulled the dish and a bottle of rye from her coat, having only just returned from a Banff sculpture retreat, and her first affair. She drank that morning; he found himself mostly listening. Because he admired her work, Jeremy was pleased that she'd given him the piece to protect it from her husband.

The hippo is hand-painted, the detail far too intricate for a child to appreciate, though no doubt it would be good to chew. The dish—the hippo's empty watering hole—is littered with fake pink roses, a fragment of dirty marble Jeremy's own father lifted from some Greek ruins when the future professor had been twelve, and some vitamin E capsules, the colour of burning bronze. The office is so chaotic that most people miss the little baroque exhibit—it's part of what Jeremy calls his lazy man's autobiography—but it has drawn the baby instantly.

Near the door is a pair of red high heels, a delicate size five, stuffed with coloured feathers. Three women in the past year have tried to slip their feet into them, but only one has bothered to put the feathers back into the shoes once she's failed to make them fit. No one has ever noticed, but high up on the bookshelf above the doorway stands a tiny caveman, about to hurl a rock. The room holds over fifteen statues and pictures of the Buddha, though they're very hard to find.

There on the screen is the young man's name.

He had taken a required composition course only a couple of semesters before. At that point at least, he hadn't declared any major.

Jeremy reads the city newspaper's obituaries on the Net.

Luke was nineteen; he's left a younger sister, parents and some unnamed others. Because he's accomplished nothing concrete, the paragraph praises his zest for life. He was quiet in class and didn't come to see Jeremy, so Jeremy doesn't know anything about Luke, though his prose, the professor remembers, showed him to be unformed, a virgin blur. Certainly the young man hadn't discovered anything so far that he could use to make his life his own.

Months later, sitting in the snow, marvelling at the light's quiet derangement, Jeremy wonders how long Luke's sister will remain damaged by that dreadful thing. Through his memory of the dead man's face, Jeremy imagines something of her high-school looks, and he hopes that he'll never find her in one of his classes.

Only a few days ago, Jeremy suspects, a terrible Christmas must have broken across Luke's family. And Mary suckled a baby whose Father had once asked another father to kill his child. And Luke will never have the chance to offer what every father must teach his son. If pressed, the best Jeremy could say would be: *Only rarely should you not fall in love.*

Have at least two bouncing bambinos. Making your baby laugh can kill cancer; and raising two children will show you how much of a desert your imagination has become.

Having just watched his wife draw her cheek across her knee, their differences opaque as usual, and about to unplug the Christmas lights, Jeremy would like to drive way, way out in the prairie, drive for hours, but the blizzard won't let him. And he wonders about useless things. Walter Benjamin once wrote that death sanctions the storyteller, that the storyteller draws authority from death. This is not something that Jeremy chooses to believe.

Jeremy's had two deaths this year. Luke in the summer and then an elderly family friend who died in a hospital bed in England; Philip, a man who should have written a memoir, but only wrote letters, mostly on aerogrammes purchased from the post office. Part of their charm was Philip's poor typing.

Jeremy had been a boy when he'd met Philip, and Philip would have been in his early fifties that night long ago, when, after returning with his wife from seeing a production of *King Lear*, he startled the young Jeremy by the relish he took in describing the scene when Gloucester is blinded. Philip had rubbed his hands together and grinned as he'd related how the man's eyes had been squished out like jam—how could an adult, a respected friend of his parents, say such things? It's only years later, whenever Jeremy teaches Aristotle, that he understands something of his beloved old friend.

Philip had taught geography in Kenya, England, the States. When she was young, his wife Susan had embroidered a map showing where he'd fought in the Second World War: arrows led from northern Africa into Italy, and then to a small concentration camp in Germany. Then further north still. Susan had looked after their first two children while Philip was off fighting in the war. They later kept the map as a screen by the electric fire. After retiring, Philip and Susan worked for an international charity, eventually visiting the Peruvian village that the organization had adopted. There they saw boats that had been destroyed by The Shining Path. Angered, but undismayed, Philip and Susan continued to believe that it was up to ordinary people to ensure that good outweighed destruction. It wasn't acceptable to try to escape from the world. That its relentless and random violence never succeeded in dispiriting them was something Jeremy found impossible to comprehend.

Philip's body gave off a singular musty and alluring smell that the boy would forever associate with Englishness. He mysteriously adored cricket. He disliked fiction because it wasn't sufficiently real, and had read much of Samuel Pepys, though the edition available to his generation was scrubbed clean of diary entries that showed how that unblinking man took his various joys. A socialist, Philip had contempt for the Beatles because of their tax-avoiding ways. Philip was a frugal man; his luxury was travel. He and Susan went everywhere, two bags between them, though he thought that the food in most countries was objectionable. On their journey in Peru they sat between the train cars, otherwise they might miss something. When travelling they wanted to know what people thought about politics, and their attitude toward religion.

The question Philip once asked a teenaged Jeremy—"what more is worth knowing than what people believe to be true and how they think they should live together?"—has stayed with Jeremy all of his life.

Before he was married, Jeremy had gone to England, and corrupt with a young man's pessimism—the world seemed utterly bereft and irredeemable—he'd been chastised by Philip for always missing the forest for the trees. When he'd died in his early nineties this past November from a stroke, Philip took, as far as Jeremy was concerned, what was good about the twentieth century with him.

Two winters from the night of the blizzard, Jeremy will take a black and white snapshot of his son shovelling snow. The photograph won't show that the shovel ends in a small rectangle of red plastic. No one will ever know that when the child was moving light scoops of snow from the driveway to the snowbank, he was hurling rocks at leopards and tigers.

But tonight Jeremy would like his rage to destroy the pull of the storm, make it heave back, just as surely as if he'd fired bullets deep and out of the family's driveway into the storm's million, billion wavering nerves.

But he's aware that his grief's too meager, his anger too easy. Thinking about loss is like trying to carve something out a waterfall. Though perhaps feeling sadness for a stranger is something that adds rather than subtracts from the world.

Jeremy wants to die before his son, though he knows that life doesn't care for categories. Life's sharp, noisy, shimmery and velvet. In bed, he lifts his wife's nightgown, its pattern based on Delft pottery, and finds warm and smiling skin.

And then later, in the foolish place between consciousness and sleep, a voice lets him know that he's the sort of man who couldn't be trusted with a dead piano.

The Fair

⸺ A whirling dervish couldn't cook and serve steak to twenty men who'd just returned from their annual summer golf tournament, but Justin hadn't stumbled. For the moment, everything was under control. Being night steward in the city's only private businessman's club demanded speed and a good memory. And it didn't hurt to gain a few allies as well. But it was having some nerves snipped that was an utter necessity: if you were thin-skinned, you wouldn't last a week.

Justin brought steak, tossed salad, a baked potato, and fresh chives to Art sitting at the bar, replaced the man's crammed ashtray. The bar was U-shaped, and when Art came by—usually once a day—he resumed his place at the bottom of the U as if he'd never been away. If he absolutely had to be out somewhere, he'd come in both before and after the meeting, social or family event—whatever it was that had made claims on his time. The owner of a men's clothing store, his only physical vanity was a thick ring with some stones in it, and a wallet that must always, always, be bloated with cash. Replacing Art's vo without asking if it was needed, Justin avoided the man's gaze—sober or drunk Art's eyes were like those of a hungry octopus that took everything in—and asked him to sign his chit. Like most of the men, Art craved company, though none of the patrons could really be called friends. If Art came by late at night and the club was empty, he was at sea. He'd quickly drink his one whisky and leave.

In the middle of filling the urinals with ice chips, Justin hurried to answer the phone.

The older club members hated telephones, so much so that they had an amendment added to the club's constitution mandating that having a cellphone go off resulted in a demerit. And after three demerits you were out. It was a Wife on the telephone, but no, her

Husband wasn't there, hadn't in fact dropped by for quite some time, and as she accused him of lying, Justin pictured a youngish woman whose stylist continuously failed to find the right tints for her hair.

Justin had been hired just before Steak Night the year before and he'd only once seen a woman make it past the door. She'd ripped into her husband over the usual things, and he'd been so humiliated after she left that he'd offered to resign.

"A new deck of cards, Justin, and a rummy pad, okay?"

Ron was going to crucify Dave in gin rummy again, and everybody knew that Dave couldn't afford it. When he'd first started the job, Justin had been amused that these men played gin rummy, a game he associated with childhood, but some of them were masters. A lot of money changed hands every night.

Davie, as he was usually called, was only a travelling salesman and he was blind to the condescension surrounding him. He rarely ran a tab, so Justin knew that he'd have to pamper him for the next hour to get any tips. After another bad game of cards, Dave would be stinging, and usually a decent enough guy, he'd still be able to gather some disdain and aim it at Justin.

Justin was worried about tomorrow. It was going to be a complicated day, but he was too busy to nail down how he felt about it. Tomorrow he'd pick up his wife Cassie, and their two girls, Shawna and Erin, to go to the summer fair. Amidst rides, sausage dogs, and trying to win some toys, they would use the day to see what it was like to do things as a family once again. He'd been living by himself since the winter.

A deteriorating marriage has its own precise and exhausted majesty, though to Justin, it seemed as if his fell apart by accident, taking him by complete surprise. Ever since he'd been a teenager, his life plan had always included Cassie.

Justin and Cassie had gone for each other in high school. He'd been in grade nine, wasn't unnecessarily humble, but still, he'd been a little baffled when this older girl from grade eleven started paying him attention. They'd met at a party, took turns shot-gunning some dope she'd brought, and after a day-long hour in her car, Cassie had announced that it was obvious he was the kind of boy who could easily lose control.

A few Saturdays later, she'd told him that her mom would be working at the department store until six. They'd both been virgins and Cassie hadn't expected the pain. But that Saturday afternoon in her narrow room and then all the others that followed grew into a time of their own.

For the rest of his life, Justin's dreams would occasionally contain some version of that second story room, a long rectangle in an old brick house that overlooked a steep river bank, a yellow room holding a distinctive smell—half adolescent female, half the dried flowers Cassie kept on her dresser—that would only come to him now when he slept.

They rarely quarrelled, and when they did it was never so bad that a frenzied phone call wouldn't return things to normal. There was the week when she had the measles and wouldn't let him see her, just sit on the floor outside her bedroom door and talk. There were the short expensive cigars she loved, for a few months anyway, that they had to smoke outside on the porch. There was that time they'd made love on the wooden walkway above the school stage while a drama class practiced *The Wizard of Oz* on the stage below.

Once when he'd accompanied Cassie and her mom to church, something Justin insisted that they do once in a while to please her, Justin came home to find a note from his own mother which teased: "Ain't Love Grand?" His mom knew how important Cassie must be to him if it got him to church, but the cheery note also saddened Justin because his mother was so utterly lonely after her divorce. During the service Cassie had giggled at the large painting of Jesus behind the pulpit emblazoned with the biblical verse "Behold, I come quickly."

"So do I," she said, playing with his fingers, "usually, but you, my sweet boy, you take an eternity."

And if each of us holds somewhere within a place so buried

and detached it seems abandoned—part grotto and part ruin—an unhurried and attentive place that stands apart from what happens on the surface, a place that pays almost no attention to the passing of time, then Cassie had somehow succeeded in entering this alcove inside Justin and she'd spray-painted her name on one of its mossy, concrete walls.

And when the fear that she would meet other guys at university threw Justin on the cool floor of nausea, he bought an engagement ring, a gift that Cassie easily accepted.

Justin quit school that spring and started serving tables full-time. The money was deceptively good because there was instantaneous cash from tips every night. The restaurant's staff was mostly composed of young people, so the job sparked some new late-night friends now that high school was over.

And then they got married, and two bright and satisfying years later it was Shawna, whose tiny and startling face was a female mask of his own. Cassie had to take fewer courses, but the daycare co-op for students helped. She got a few hours a week working at the library. Two more years passed and it had been a long time since it was customary for Justin to have some people over after work on Saturday nights. When they first married, going back to get his high-school diploma was something that Justin always promised to do next year, but now it had become impossible.

But it didn't matter because when he'd come home from work he'd glow to see Shawna's bottle in the fridge waiting for her if she woke, and sometimes he'd sit on the bathroom floor in the dark and just take in her bath toys tumbled with Cassie's moccasins by the tub.

Joining Cassie in bed, some nights he'd find her a wave of greed, that lovely kind that usually only came about after they'd returned home very late from a party and didn't want the night to end. More often than not when he entered their bedroom she was already sleeping and sometimes she'd be in her light blue pajamas, the ones with the stars he'd given her on her first Mother's Day. And she'd be filling the darkness with her sleep, filling his mind with words that utterly enchanted him—*her* and *she*.

After a while, something told Cassie that she needed another baby. When Erin eventually came, Cassie dropped her all of her classes except one film course. Justin turned twenty-three and he applied for the job at the men's club because working there would broaden his experience.

Then the part-time steward at the club quit, which left the Saturday shift available. You opened up at eleven in the morning, closed at eight. They needed the money, and Justin insisted that he would pick up the extra hours.

"But I get lonely for you as it is," Cassie had finally said, trying to close down the argument, "and so do the kids."

"Don't try to make me feel guilty."

And then one late Sunday afternoon, deep in a cold snap that kept the whole city indoors for over a week, Shawna developed an earache that made her scream with an intensity of pain she'd never encountered before. All four of them had the flu. When the earache struck, every hour or so, it knocked Shawna off her chair on to the floor. Cassie took her to a walk-in clinic, and Justin knew that the antibiotics would take up most of that Saturday's tips.

While they were out, Erin wouldn't stay in her Winnie the Pooh plush chair and watch a video. They'd watched a dozen kids' videos all day and she was bored. Wandering around while her father polished his shoes, she eventually discovered herself beside the bathtub. She tried to flush her dolphins down the toilet, and two of them got through, blocking the plumbing, but Justin didn't know this when he later needed to use the bathroom. Instead, he fished the remaining dolphins out of the bowl, reprimanded Erin, and sat down. The toilet inevitably overflowed and when Cassie returned Justin was hysterical. He tried to send the girls to bed, but they hadn't been fed and bathed yet. Shawna's cry erupted again, which spread to Erin.

"I can't fucking stand this life," Justin screamed, his hands curled around the top of a kitchen chair, the savage, courageous words breaking out after he'd been trying hard, so utterly hard to keep them inside.

Fortunately he'd been secretly banking some of his tips in a separate account, just in case something like this happened.

In the winter the bar was less busy, so Justin frequently had time to play a clumsy game of snooker in the club's game room upstairs. Chalking up the cue, surveying the coloured balls, predicting their trajectories and combinations, Justin was a man who belonged. Sometimes he'd talk to himself in various accents as he made his shots. But then the door would ring downstairs and somebody would be seated at the bar ready to be served.

But that was okay—because ultimately snooker was boring.

One he'd been throwing darts upstairs when he heard the bell. Skipping down the stairs, he straightened his loosened tie, only to find someone he didn't recognize at the bar. After several months on the job, Justin thought he'd met everyone, but the man looking at him couldn't have been a member.

He hadn't removed his coat, a shabby parka thick with snow, and his face wasn't right.

When the fellow wouldn't leave immediately Justin told him he'd be forced to call the police, but the bastard just laughed.

"It'll take them awhile to get here, don't you think, in this storm?"

"We'll see. Look, you can't stay. I'll get in shit if a member comes and finds you here."

"Hold your horses, I just want a beer."

"I can't do that."

"Sure you can. The sooner I have my drink, the sooner I'm gone."

"What kind do you want?"

"Oh, a Pilsner will do."

"That's three dollars."

"Here's five, something for you."

"Drink it fast."

"You shouldn't talk to me like that."

"Listen, I'm the one doing you a favour."

"No, you listen to me. I'm just a cook, but that's my business. I was just passing by. I got off work early on account of the snow, had a couple of beers up at Duffy's. I've always wanted to come in here. But nobody ever invited me."

"It's a private club. Members only."

"Who cares? I can drink beer as well as they can. Tell me something"

"What do you want to know?"

"How old are you?"

"The right age."

"Good for you. And Lordee, I'm the wrong age. But Mister, I'll tell you something. Do you want to know what fear is? Don't look like that, I'm not going to jump over the bar."

"Why should I be afraid of you?"

"You're too young. You couldn't possibly know real fear. None of the pricks who come in here have any idea."

"Finish your beer."

"No, I'll have one more. Here's another five."

Justin rang in the beer, but still, sweat stuck to his shirt when he turned his back to the old man.

"I was in the Merchant Marine in the war. Our ship got sunk in the north Atlantic. You don't know cold either. I had to jump in the water. We all did. Christ Almighty, what do you know? Fire's ripping across the waves, it's the oil, sucks all the air away. Finally, one of our ships goes by, trailing life preservers. I got one, most of the other guys didn't. If I'd been in the water any longer it wouldn't have mattered anymore."

"That's quite a story. But tell you what—I've got a job to keep. I've got kids at home. And a wife."

"I've got three kids, somewhere."

"I can squeeze off a whiskey for you. How's that? Then you have to go."

"Make it scotch."

"Scotch it is," Justin said, reaching for the bar brand.

"No, make it a good one, you got some Johnnie Walker Black?"

But as soon as he slid the empty shot glass back across the bar, the night's drinking took the old man suddenly, like a mudslide. His fire caved in, disappeared under the avalanche, as if it had never been, and the world collapsed around him, closing him in. He made his way to the rarely used front door, muttering something. The last thing Justin saw of him were his hands struggling to get at his hood.

Justin had told Cassie about the man when he'd gotten home that night, though he'd never mentioned the incident to anyone at the club because he thought there might be trouble.

Working in a bar, each night, each week blurs into the next one, so it wasn't long until Justin had forgotten the incident.

There was a roar from upstairs and soon Dave—down seventy bucks from playing gin—was beside the bar letting everyone know that Brad was cleaning up in the craps game. Already, he'd won over two thousand. Dave was giddy with watching other guys lose.

Hearing about Brad's success, the club's only jeweller reminded everyone that he'd paid no taxes the previous year, but the boast was stale.

The club members patronized each other's businesses, sought and found corroboration against the outside world amongst each other, made financial recommendations, but nothing linked them so much as the shared understanding that the ongoing purpose of reality was to let the better man win.

Motioning for another VO, Art declared from out of the blue that women should be kept in cages.

But the others ignored him as they gathered their drinks to go upstairs and see how long Brad, the owner of a construction company, a man who didn't come to the club that often, could keep up his winning streak.

Justin wasn't surprised by Art's remark, though he was aggravated that he'd have to keep going upstairs to check on everybody's drinks. What did take him back was how stupid these guys were about sex, how stuck they were on the same topics. And yet they fascinated him too. Completely different from the people who lived in Justin's world, they were predators with an enormous sense of will. What they wanted usually became theirs.

There was Bill, who'd had one kidney removed thirty years before. He didn't drink because of this but he still kept up his membership dues, coming in to the club several times a week to have a ginger ale or club soda and read his newspaper. Shortly after he'd first met Justin, he'd seen fit to warn him of how disgusting it was to go down on a woman.

Bill was generally treated with respect, but he'd repeatedly piss off the younger guys by telling them that in his heyday he could put them all under the table. They knew nothing about whisky he told them. He'd call them pussy-lickers and then announce, as if for the first time, that "you can't knock them up with spit."

The older men tended to agree. Oral sex, they held, was for guys who couldn't get it up.

They used to consult Justin about his wife's tastes, but he'd shrug his shoulders.

Once Art had suggested that Justin had probably left his wife so he could suck his boyfriend's cock—but then George had cut in, telling Art that he was just jealous that Justin was a free man. Not only that, he'd added, Art probably hadn't even seen his dick in ten years, let alone used it.

Art responded with a lame, "fuck off."

Justin was grateful for George, except that he would try to transfix him in monologues about how his daughters wouldn't talk to him until he quit drinking. The family pictures would come out, and the tips would get better and better, but George wanted to own Justin's time, something that he couldn't afford.

They'd have fired Justin if they'd known about some of the things that he'd done when only one other person was looking.

Later, when he left after midnight, three thousand plus some IOUs in hand, Brad slipped a fifty in Justin's shirt pocket, money that would help pay for kids' rides the next day. Eventually it was time to offer last call, clean up, count the cash, and tally the receipts. Turn off the lights. This was the best time. Even though he had to stay awhile to balance the cash, Justin would open his one free beer, and soak in the freedom of closing down the bar.

When the club was empty after last call, it took on an identity it was denied during regular hours. Despite the pictures of dogs playing poker on the walls, the club grew a surly dignity. The tools of leisure became aloof. The bottles of liquor, even the tape on the carpet in front of the dartboards marking where a player should stand, the side tables made to hold drinks—each object threw off its own aura of rancour.

Justin knew he was tolerated, but only for so long.

If the almost three hundred nights Justin had worked in the club were rolled into one busy, busy shift, and if an abrupt failure of the electricity made everything vanish into darkness, and if the bar was suddenly bereft of movement and all bodily tissue, this is what would appear:

Various flames—all different in intensity, colour, even smell.

The once savagely handsome, self-styled aristocratic owner of a famous brand of shirts, a bitterly lonely man who'd never met anyone he didn't scorn, especially the other club members, whose manners and palpable ignorance disgusted him—this man's flame is blunt with fury and the absurd pride he takes in ironing his own clothes.

Beside him a turquoise hiss like an acetylene torch.

The darkness threatens to douse Dave the salesman's few sparks.

Art is the colour of gasoline on water, though with an almost jet black, peacock green that, sizzling as it burns, spits out gobs of oily light that cling in the air.

George is a handheld mirror set alight.

These men believe in being socially relevant—they know that the world can't function without them—and they are bathed in a cloud of wet, pastel grey, the slow shape of their contempt. Which is sleepless.

If Justin could envision the flickering bar, he would recognize the purity, the ravenous clarity of some of its flames, the awkwardness of others, but he wouldn't be able to make out his own form, a bright carelessness igniting the space around him.

Because he needed to pick up the girls for the fair in a little over eight hours, Justin drove home, had a couple of beers, tried channel surfing to wind down, and went to bed.

When they went by the *Titanic* the first time it wasn't very busy. The huge inflated slide was angled at about thirty-five degrees, safe enough to let Shawna fling herself down past the smokestacks, skid without becoming frightened to the pads below. Other rides more exciting to the girls had followed, but after a few hours Justin was impatient to leave Kiddy Land. The fair was crowded with beautiful women.

Justin had been taking pictures of their day together, occasionally framing his shots so that along with the kids, they also included something nice as she bent over to tie a shoe. Or stood talking on her cell, flicking a cigarette with long fingers joined to a perfect arm with bangles. Or just simply the black woman with folded arms, golden hair, looking at him. And the colour of her nail polish, an odd silver the camera would never pick up; her toenails glinted like fish scales beneath fluorescent lights.

He shot five pictures of Cassie and the girls on the Ferris wheel. They'd been going by too quickly for him to see their faces, but the camera caught the concentration in Cassie's smile, her left arm around the children, the astonishment filling Shawna as they spun, then rocked above the fair grounds. In one of the instants Justin clicked the camera, Erin was thoroughly lost in something she could see somewhere over there. He also shot a picture of a father with his brain-damaged daughter, she turned to one side with long, long hair and he with a look that showed too many years of being the solitary caretaker.

And later, about to whip 'round the curve of the track in stubby racecar, Shawna and Erin's faces were locked into the unfathomable, continuously unbroken surprise of childhood, safe there in the immediately forgotten.

Erin had seen gargoyles, ghosts, and dragons on TV, but there was something bad about the man way up high in the castle so she found something else to watch—then Shawna shouted at her Mommy to look at the skeleton, it's a real skeleton.

If he'd been alive the statue would have surveyed a sauntering crowd made up of teenagers and little families; individuals were present for a moment and then they disappeared. As things were, the skeleton gripped a sickle that spasmodically cut through the sky, the quiet air that was moist with the rain that would fall later that afternoon.

And all the while Justin and Cassie were talking. Mostly about the kids. Though she did bring him back to the times when they'd come to the same fair as teenagers. She'd known there was a chance that he didn't want to remember things like that, but he'd reacted by putting his arm around her.

Soon after, Erin began weeping her heart away because she wasn't tall enough to go on a dragon ride. Her sobs became screams, and Justin immediately vanished behind his eyes. He forced himself to recognize that they'd grow out of these crying jags. They got Erin settled by telling her that she could go on the Ferris wheel again. On their way there, a man in his forties waved at Cassie, calling her by name.

"Who's that?"

"His name's Tom. He goes to the support group I go to. He's with his son. Look."

"Support group?"

"It's for single parents, or people who've just got divorced."

"We're not divorced."

"I know, honey, and I don't want to be either."

"So he must be thinking to himself: there goes her husband the asshole."

"It's not like that. Everyone was happy we were going to have the day together."

"Everyone? You told this entire so-called support group about today?"

"Justin, I don't know what to do. Do you have any idea what it's like to go for days and not talk to an adult? I'm falling apart Justin. Sometimes I cry so hard at night that I put a towel over my head so the kids can't hear me."

"It's okay, Cassie, it's okay."

"Is it really? Are you coming home?"

"I didn't mean that. I just meant—"

"Then how can things be okay? I just can't stand that you have all the power. Everything depends upon you."

Justin stopped himself from saying that he didn't go to any support group. That he didn't talk to anyone about their private problems.

"I made a lot of money in tips last night, let's let the kids have fun."

"You too, okay."

"No problem there, Cassie."

The local rock station provided a shining jeep decorated with fake graffiti, a multiplex of grey, almost black speakers, free balloons and glow-in-the-dark Frisbees. Two DJs were working, one of whom could have won a Dennis Hopper look-alike contest.

As Justin went by pushing the double stroller, both kids having become tired, the DJs started playing a song that was popular that summer.

Its lyrics were mostly spoken, a kind of dissipated rap, but the background vocals belonged to a falling, endlessly rising angel, who tried to let the crowd in on something that she felt was necessary to know. From some studio far away, her voice had somehow become a rich graze against the overcast sky, making ordinary words pass through the skin.

A water slide called Niagara Falls had one of the longest lineups and Shawna, who kept herself tightly by Justin's side, pointed out that the "S" in the sign was broken. It was true—all the other yellow bulbs making up the words worked.

It was also true that Cassie sometimes cried under a towel. She'd even started smoking again that winter when Justin had left, just so she had an excuse to go outside and be alone for a few minutes. She'd plop Shawna and Erin in front of the TV, give them some juice, and then she'd sit on the steps to the townhouse long enough to smoke one cigarette. She kept a spaghetti sauce tin in the window well for the butts. When the nights became warmer and the girls were sleeping, she'd go outside and try to find privacy on the steps so she could work things over.

But you can't be alone in a townhouse complex.

Though he never directed a word in her direction, one of Cassie's neighbours was always watching her. She could see him stuffing his mind with images as he worked on his lawn and flowers. Though the lawn was actually his mother's. A few of the townhouses had been sold as condos, and this man's mother lived across from Cassie and the girls. Cassie didn't know either of them because they felt superior to the renters and kept to themselves.

The man was utterly fastidious on his hands and knees in his rubber boots, keeping the grass an emerald and disciplined sea, while he nurtured the marigolds lining the sidewalk into botanical soldiers who would keep ants and beetles away. One night Cassie had caught him behind binoculars. He'd been wrapped in his mother's living room curtains, in the dark, looking up into her bedroom window.

When she could, Cassie would read on the steps outside, ignoring the world. She'd always been a reader, and even now she forced herself—no matter how tired the day had made her—to find some time to read. The longer the book the better because she liked to get to know the characters, feel the way they saw things. When she found writers she liked, she'd binge on them. A couple of years ago it'd been Amy Tan—who was almost too sad to read—and then it was some D.H. Lawrence, most of Thomas Harris. Stephen King was slumming but addictive all the same. She'd been into Anaïs Nin when she was seventeen and decided that she wanted to lose her virginity with Justin.

She'd been just about to start an Anne Rice novel the weekend Justin had had his meltdown, which, had she read it, would have led into a long dive into her stuff, except that Shawna and Erin had gotten sick. The book went back to the library unread.

Shawna had taken Justin's absence the worst. She'd regressed at first, and still had to be cured of the impulse to put everything in her mouth. She'd lost her concentration, couldn't even stay still for bedtime stories. She needed Cassie to lie in bed with her until she fell asleep. And Cassie hated Justin for what he'd made her become; all her daughters would see of her was an exhausted and bitter woman. It simply wasn't fair.

Mornings were full of the kids, trying to figure out how to fill the day without spending money. Mornings meant hoping for an afternoon nap. Nighttime was always the worst, when the girls were sleeping and when she couldn't avoid a mood that combined self-pity and self-righteousness, a treacherous emotional cocktail that resulted only in numbness if she was lucky. Then she could merely phase out watching TV.

Throughout the months, an unrelenting depression nestled more deeply inside her. She became narrower and narrower. If she ever acted like Justin did, she was the bad mother—why did he get to walk away, stranding her, leaving her with every single responsibility? His selfishness was incomprehensible.

That Cassie couldn't afford to buy books anymore was yet another thorn. She could easily summon the rage from the day a month before when she'd had to sell her books to buy two stupid bags of groceries, but she distrusted anger, having seen enough of it when she was younger.

Justin liked movies more than books. They'd seen hundreds and hundreds of movies together. One of the things she'd resented about his job at the men's club was that it took away their movie time. It was just a little thing, but one of the reasons she loved him was that he was perfect to watch a movie with.

And when they'd been teenagers he'd understood what it meant to have to take care of a parent. They both had mothers to look after; even now, Cassie's mom, Lee, was frantic to know what was wrong if they didn't talk on the phone once a day.

When he'd first started going with Cassie, Justin had recognized that he'd have to woo his girlfriend's mother. And he'd succeeded so well that Lee had been tempted to blame her daughter for the separation. But only tempted. Lee knew for a fact that there wasn't a man in the world who hadn't become emotionally stalled somewhere around seventeen.

But reading didn't feel the same to Cassie anymore. Anticipation of any kind just seemed too demanding, and sometimes it proved dangerous. And exhaustion was eating her, cell by cell from the inside. She lost even more weight—two bra sizes disappeared. She knew that if she gave into this life, she would sleep until the girls were teenagers, so she had her mom babysit one night a week so she could take up something new. Or just get away for a few hours.

Belly dancing lessons were strangely fun for a few weeks, but too expensive. Sometimes she'd go to a movie down at the library. Every so often she'd take a vacation from being a mother, and go with a girlfriend to a bar and drink gin and tonics.

One Saturday night she'd spent the evening drinking with Justin and his best friend, Gerry, at Gerry's apartment. After a few hours, Justin had succeeded in getting Gerry to neck with her, but she soon called a taxi because she didn't like where things were headed. She needed to talk to someone who was sane, but when she got home, her mom was asleep on the couch. What tore into Cassie was that she needed to let loose about how weird her life was becoming, but it was always Justin who was the only person in the world with whom she ever really cared to talk.

Before he'd left, she'd hated that he'd been working so hard, and she'd known that winter in a small townhouse was punishing all of them, but still, she'd been astonished when he'd had that fit in February, and that he'd actually chosen to leave. That Saturday night, the night before he left, they'd been able to steer away from frustration with careful, inspired play.

While they'd been putting away the girls' toys, Justin had picked up a plastic telephone and phoned her while sitting on the floor. She was supposed to call an ambulance because being surrounded by the colours of kids' toys was going to give him an aneurysm.

Why hadn't she seen any of this coming?

But she'd called him back on the other toy phone, Erin's, and they'd managed to make a game out of the two of them sitting in a messy living room with kids' phones in their hands.

Cassie usually had a sense of how things were, not only for her family, but for other people too. One look at somebody's face was all she needed. She'd seen the slow turning world of Justin's patience when he'd been more a boy than a man. It didn't seem possible that she'd been missing what had been going on in her husband's mind for at least a year now.

When he left his family, the punishing cold had kept on for another week. Closing up the bar, Justin would hear trees cracking in the night—they sounded like random rifle shots fired across the empty streets. He'd rented a bachelor apartment close to the club because Cassie was right that she needed the car more than he did. Walking to his apartment, he felt his earring freeze against his skin. Clusters of icicles exploded.

Flush with tips and his changed life, he eventually began stopping into an after-hours club. It was a pleasure to be a customer for a change. If you slipped the server something she'd bring you a beguiling inch of Jack Daniels in a Styrofoam cup. And with almost no effort, the months became that summer night which would become an afternoon at the fair.

Before he'd gone to sleep that Thursday night before the fair, Justin had sat on his bed, his skin wet against the wall, and tried to think. More than anything, he needed to launch some probes out into wherever it was that his elemental self lived. He needed to determine what it really knew, and felt, what it simply had to have. But it was impossible to decide. He was exhausted; his shift at the club seemed to have held a few more hours than usual. He'd made the uncommonly large sum of one hundred and sixty-seven dollars in tips, probably enough to provide a good day for the girls at the fair—but he had no real idea as to what his life required from him.

And if being separate from his family presented him with the unfamiliar feelings of guilt and grief, the severity of which he hadn't been expecting, the first time he'd undressed a woman who wasn't Cassie he was entirely unprepared to find that everything had instantly shifted. Because Cassie had been his only lover, it probably meant that all of his life was as narrow as his sexual experience. And how could it not be true that with each year he'd been steadily confining himself more and more?

So he'd gotten an earring, and bought some new music. He'd sampled coke twice, but recognized its danger, so stayed away from it after that. He bought some stolen electronics, including a computer that he didn't care to tell Cassie about. They already had one at home. But he could justify the purchase because if he decided to move home again, he'd give it to Shawna and buy her some CD ROMs.

He decorated the apartment with René Magritte paintings that he'd got for half-price in a calendar sale. The whole year surrounded him on the walls. He disciplined himself to eat two meals a day, which was hard. He was rarely hungry.

Once, just to see, he'd honestly tried to make it with a man. But it hadn't worked out very well.

He'd enjoyed that a man's kisses were rougher than a woman's, and found facial stubble a turn-on. And although holding another man's cock was exciting, giving head wasn't. His lover told Justin that he should stick to pussy, and after they'd done some shooters of tequila, the bastard poured some tequila in Justin's fish tank, almost instantly killing his prized cichlids.

Then he met April on the Net. They went to a Sunday matinee movie, stopped into a restaurant for mussels, pasta, and house wine, and to his surprise she agreed to come back to his apartment for some more drinks. And all the while Justin was careful not to get involved with someone who could pull him away from Cassie.

April was a university student who lived at home and, unlike the others who insisted on condoms, she let him ride bare back. They only went to one more movie after that because it suited both of them more just to go to his apartment.

"I'm haunted," she'd told him late one Saturday night. She was sitting on his bed, drinking a thick vodka Justin kept for her in his freezer.

"And this means?"

"There's something dark, I don't know what it is exactly, but it lives in my room at home. It's probably no bigger than my fingernail, but it's cruel and always watches me. And it follows me; it knows how to find me, wherever I go."

"Is it here?"

"No, not yet," she said, taking in the small room, the pictures on the wall, the CDs on the floor, the toys he kept in a box for when the girls came over. Justin was sitting tight on a wooden chair, his arms around his knees, and he watched her stir the remaining ice cube in her glass.

"Has it ever been here?"

"No, and that's very, very weird. It's always found me before."

"What does it look like?"

"I don't know. It just takes over an object, sort of fills it up, and lets me know it's there."

"Does it always stay in the same place?"

"Oh, it's got its favourites for sure, but no, it doesn't stay anywhere for long."

"What's one of its favourites?"

"I've got one of those garden statues in my room, like a Greek goddess. She's holding a jug for wine. It likes her."

"Why do you think it hasn't come here."

"Maybe it's you."

"It doesn't like me you mean?"

"Justin, do you love me?"

"No."

"Do you at least like me?"

"That I know for sure—can't you tell?"

"Would you let me move in with you?"

"April, don't do this."

"I don't mind that you have kids."

"Let me get you some more vodka."

When he was standing in front of the freezer, she asked him from the open bathroom whether he actually liked surrealism.

"Sometimes," Justin said, though he didn't know exactly what she was talking about.

"Tell you what, I want you to do something for me," April said, having taken his place on the armchair.

"Go ahead."

"Sometime in the future I'll probably be married, say ten years from now. I want you to come and get me, kidnap me. I want you to tie me up and then play with me."

"How am I supposed to find you in ten years?"

"Trust me, if I know you, you'll find a way."

Later she took a long, blue scarf from her backpack and blindfolded him. After a while, she got on top, and then Justin heard something that could only be what it was, the sound of metal against skin. She was rubbing a fishing knife against her nipples.

"April, what the hell?"

The night before the fair Cassie had sat on the step, first with the girls, and she'd painted everyone's nails, sixty nails in three different colours, and after they'd gone to sleep, she looked at the future and tried hard not to curl away from it—the future seemed to have already abandoned her as it took everyone, even Justin and the girls, to some other place. But that was loser thinking, something that was almost impossible to fight. And worse, there was the sickening possibility that you could only fall in love once. She thought about doing some laundry because even in her hardest moments, hanging up her daughter's clothing thrilled her.

But she couldn't move.

She forced her mind to stay focused on the blue-black sky.

If she sat still long enough, the night would breathe through her skin and find another sky inside her, the real one, the one that would keep her from going down into the basement and start howling like an animal.

The rain started at the fair soon after the girls had eaten candy floss, a few warm drops on their arms, each about the size of a bee sting. They saw a boy lose three balloons to the restless, blackening wind. Erin was almost asleep. But Shawna wanted more, more rides Mommy. Justin had only two hours before he had to get to work so it was decided that he would push Erin back to the car and Cassie would take Shawna for one more ride.

They returned to the dragon roller coaster and after their ride, Shawna started to vomit and Cassie's hands felt good on her small shoulders for a little while and then Mommy sat her down on a bench and because Erin's diaper wipes were in the stroller, Mommy went to get some napkins, and then hurrying back Cassie was struck hard on one shoulder, then the other by two men going the opposite directions.

Her bag was gone. The men got a bottle of coated Aspirin, an Air Miles coupon, some water, Justin's camera, and her wallet. Inside the wallet was the money Justin had given her for the next two weeks. At least she'd given him her car keys.

Sitting in the car with his sleeping daughter, Justin had almost fallen asleep himself when he glimpsed Cassie carrying Shawna coming toward him through the parking lot. Something was obviously wrong. What had he done wrong now? He got out of the car and met them.

Never had he seen his wife that way. He'd seen Cassie cry before but he'd never seen tears on a face so alive with fear.

Justin knew he had no choice but to say that he'd come home for good after work that night. He would, he would return home to where he belonged. Later, when he had time away from customers at the bar, he phoned twice to check on the girls, and as he drove home around two-thirty he felt like a hero, though a very uncertain hero.

From seven to eight that night, though, he'd been enraged that chance had ruined his new life, had hurled him from one world to another, but as his shift wore on he began to feel gentler, more assured, though the hours continued to spin just beyond his grasp. It was impossible to feel that he was part of himself.

After the aggravation of phoning credit card companies, getting the girls settled, cleaning up, at midnight Cassie found herself jubilant, and enraged, relieved too, but mostly bewildered and all scraped up inside. Lying on the couch between going out to smoke, drinking tea, absurdly wondering what to wear, worrying that Justin's decision to come home had been forced and wouldn't last, she finally gave up, and just waited for Justin to come home, hoping that eventually the night would simply become ordinary to her.

As she went to sleep after she and Justin had talked and talked, and after she'd turned off the purple blue night light to the sound of robins waking, Cassie reminded herself to throw out the condoms she'd bought and hidden in her jewellery box just on the odd chance that she might sometime bring a man home.

The next day was a Saturday and Cassie had let Justin sleep in before he had to go to work. He told the girls that he'd be home in time to read them bedtime stories. Because he knew how much his girlfriend April despised living in her childhood bedroom,

Justin phoned her from work, and asked if she wanted to sublet his apartment. It was time for him to return to his family. He'd give his month's notice for the apartment, get his deposit back, and she could live rent-free for what was left of this month. It was a great deal—what did she think? Tell you what, he said, they could split the following month's rent, and then she could decide what she wanted to do. He'd pick her up; he had his car back again. She just needed to give him her address.

They agreed to meet after he finished work.

The day dragged; it was cottage season and the bar wasn't very busy. Tips were low. But then Art came in, and after his VO and a couple of cigarettes it all came out. There'd been a meeting of the club's board members that afternoon; an anonymous member had complained to City Hall about the club's non-existent smoking policies.

After another VO, and arguing that the club was private property, Art spat out in rage: "This club, this sanctuary, is doomed because some bitch lawyer is going to sue us. Our membership requirements are allegedly discriminatory."

"Well you guys would know what to do with her if she ever came through the door," Justin offered.

Something cruel gleamed in Art's eyes—the delight of giving pain.

"You better start thinking about getting a new job," he told Justin.

"Why? What have I done?"

"It's not you. You do a passable job. But there's no way in hell we're going to allow cunts to become members. We'll close first. And that means that you, my friend, will be out of work. Be better to burn the place down than let pussies in."

Justin was going to ask Art if he could get a job in one of his stores, but the idea of working under him was nauseating.

"Christ, Art," Justin said, "I bet this woman lawyer wants to sit on your bar stool. Take it over. Wonder if she drinks VO?"

"What are you saying?"

"Nothing Art," Justin said, and tilted the bottle of whiskey.

Art nodded.

After Art had left, Justin felt empty and rebellious, afraid for the future, and angry that he'd stayed with this job for so long. Just before he closed up he tucked two bags of potato chips in his jacket, something for Shawna and Erin.

Driving to April's place, Justin was preoccupied with Art's bad news and he drove through a red light. And when he found April's street, he hadn't counted on how uncomfortable it was going to be to meet her parents. But there she was, sitting on the curb in front of the house. With a new ring in her eyebrow, a backpack, and a T-shirt she'd designed herself, April pretended to be hitchhiking as he pulled up the car.

At first, it was hard to talk to her. Justin didn't want to mention his new problem, and so he gave in to the moment. See what happened. Because it was going to be her apartment, April wanted the keys. He told her he needed to get some of his things. Upstairs, those small, uncomfortably hot rooms were now only a parenthesis in his life. Despite his worries, Justin felt good that he was finally doing the right thing.

He'd spent an hour with April when he'd had the inspiration to order some Indian food—Cassie's favourite. It would buy him some time. He took April to the restaurant, bought her a drink, and then phoned Cassie and told her where he was, that the place was busy and he'd be home with a late night dinner as soon as he could.

"Do you really know what you're doing?" April asked him, stirring her drink, as they waited for the food.

"How could I?"

"Don't be an asshole, what kind of answer is that?"

"I mean it, I don't know."

"Are you going to ever stop by the Absinthe for a drink now that you're a family man again?"

"Now and then."

"And your wife won't mind?"

"It's not like that."

"What's not like that?"

"She doesn't have a punch clock on the door for when I come home."

"What makes you so certain?"

"I just know."

"Have you told her about me?"

"No."

"What do you expect me to do?"

"Come on, you know as well as I do that I'm not the only guy in your life."

"Promise me two things, Justin, only two things. You'll pay me a visit in ten years and you won't turn out like those businessmen you've told me about."

Justin nodded, though he had no intention of seeing April again. Looking directly at her, he wondered if, when she met new men in the future, she would continue to tell them that she was haunted.

"You're always going to love me, you know that, don't you?" April said.

Justin stayed in the car when he dropped April off from the restaurant. She waved in her odd way, and then went upstairs with the take-out meal he'd insisted on buying for her. There wasn't a lot in the fridge but there was all that she'd need for a while.

It was going to be heavenly not to have to face another human being for two or three days.

When Justin had called late that morning, April had thought he'd wanted to her to come over after he got off work and screw, and she was going to say no. Just to see how he'd react. Hilarious that she'd ended up in the apartment all the same. She picked up the phone and there were some messages that she erased. She told one of the Magritte pictures that things were going to change before she tore it down off of the wall.

Eating with her fingers, she felt alone in herself in a promising way. It was early in the night as far as she was concerned. Nights could be endless. The vodka Justin kept for her in the freezer was still there.

April had had a revelation of sorts when she'd woken up that morning. An inspiration. She'd realized that her life had become one of those lives that people would like to hear about, so now, alone in her new apartment, she looked at her life and turned on her mini-cassette tape recorder. She started talking and making notes. She wasn't all that jumpy anymore; she felt so serene she could easily slide out of her skin, and she had so much that people needed to find out. And finally, some ninety minutes later, she began to wear out, but the words still kept coming. It was impossible—all those words— but they simply wouldn't stop as they pushed her back further and further, way past the many things that attacked her.

April knew that the demon that had chosen her, her of all the people she knew couldn't control her anymore. What mattered was freedom, and April knew she could finally begin to be free. And freedom didn't touch everyone. No one, certainly not Justin, could ever begin to understand. April knew she was that branch of lightning that illuminated the darkness.

Encounters

— Lying in bed, Jenn closed her eyes to Guatemala, the volcanoes in the distance, the red cotton scarf she'd been given at a festival, the smell of her last Cadbury chocolate bar from the case a friend back home had sent her. She didn't want to go, but she was about to begin leaving Guatemala that night. In only a few hours, she'd be on a four AM bus to Guatemala City. Once there, she'd take a week to look around parts of the country she hadn't seen yet before flying home.

For the past several months, Jenn had been a volunteer in a Guatemalan orphanage. When she wasn't at the orphanage, she worked in a movie house to make some money, hiked up volcanoes, considered going scuba diving off El Salvador, took pictures.

She was living with an older man, Martin, who laughed at jokes only he could understand. Everyone would just stare at the floor avoiding him when he told his wacky, completely unintelligible stories. Sometimes he'd help at the orphanage. He also had a Buddha tattoo. That a big man would make himself seem even heavier with a fat Buddha spreading over his torso had been what had made her curious about him in the first place.

Martin slept face down, pressing the large laughing Buddha that tattooed his hairless chest and stomach into the sheets. He kept opening and closing his fingers.

So this is what it means to have a Buddha for a lover, she thought, but she didn't know what exactly *this* was, only that it wasn't going to continue. She still hadn't decided whether she'd let Marty come with her to the airport to see her off.

It was cold, and she turned toward him, lying on her right side, away from the wall. Ever since she'd been a child, she'd known that spiders come at you from the wall, and while it was also true that monsters launch their attacks through the doorway, she preferred monsters to spiders.

What meant the most was working on the unfinished garden. No, what meant most was the makeshift family of volunteers, not the ones who breezed in and out, making, then breaking promises, what mattered most were the few who stayed for months, grew committed to that miserable building, its terraced hill, the kids. These dedicated volunteers gave her a sense of belonging she'd never had before.

At first, she'd castigated herself for making the trip to Guatemala— it was such a cliché. Young woman—make that restless, arrogant and inexperienced young white woman—visits poor country to straighten herself out. And it was true, the peasants slaved for Green Giant and Delmonte. She'd never eat canned fruit again. And untrustworthy, tattered dogs chased pigs, sometimes got run over and then were just left there in the streets, and little boys got stoned on glue, their dark eyes burnt into shells, and the dirt gave her appalling rashes, scalded her with explosions of diarrhea. But feeling bad about hypocrisy was just another form of self-indulgence, and she was utterly sick of mind games, especially her own.

So she worked harder at the orphanage, became recognized by people in the street, and despite being the oldest volunteer was called *la nina*, took pictures, enjoyed when someone from British Columbia recognized her special made-only-in-Vancouver Taiga pants, became tanned, watched a lot of bad movies at the cinema she ran at nights, discovered new, but usually bearable, kinds of loneliness, threw away pictures, eventually became *Nino* Jenn, had frequent arguments with a priest as she demanded more money for the orphanage, promised herself that she'd learn how to become loyal to reality.

This is an e-mail she sent to a friend back home in Canada:

hi, it's me, finally. it's late & i've just dropped by the only open computer cafe for a few minutes before hitting the hay. i just got off work at the cinema. tonite i had to show one of those Stallone Rambo films. my mood's better now. being depressed happens to all of us 'long termers' here. we ask ourselves questions like "do you have the dilemma of needing another pair of pants but not wanting to own them?" Things are better here than when i arrived. When i first came, i'd be here on a Sunday morning when the kids were at church and everything was disgusting. Diapers dirtying the floor, crushed and spilled food everywhere, chicken dihoreah (?), bugs. Once i had to make lunch for 53 kids who would be arriving from church in two hours, v. v. hungry. nothing in the fridge but a few carrots with decayed leaves, potatoes, one onion, some beans, and a pumpkin. So i made soup. A while later, Sylvie, a woman from Germany, showed up carrying a crying baby who'd been eating dirt, cry, cry, cry— i've discovered that crying children drive me insane. But i'll learn.

i could type for hours, but am sleepy. Catch some dragonflies for me and send them in a bottle with air holes because there's too many mosquitoes at night

jenn

p.s. could you go to Chapters and see if they have __I, Rigoberta Menchu: an Indian Woman in Guatemala__ because it's v.v. expensive here. Thanks.

She could have fallen for John the Australian, the most well-read person she'd ever met, someone who understood precisely why she was in Guatemala. It was so rare that she met men who truly intrigued her. But he too was adrift, and wouldn't start anything. He told her she should start by reading Borges; but he wouldn't sleep with her because they both needed their independence. Fine, she respected this; she could become the sort of friend he wanted her to be. But then he hooked up with Ashley from Louisiana—you could hear them fucking like bunnies at night—and eventually the two of them left to march with the Zapatistas.

John had introduced her to Marty, the nicest of guys, John claimed. John was partially right about Marty, but Jenn suspected he'd been feeling guilty and had been trying to get her involved with somebody else. Nearly forty, exiled from the States because he'd been busted for selling alcohol to minors, Marty with the compulsively cleaned fingernails—Marty, the Buddha. It had taken a few weeks, but he'd been relentless in his pursuit of her.

One night she'd come home from the cyber café and someone had placed a canary yellow bikini on her bed. Two goldfish were swimming in a bowl on her night table. There was a note and a tape recorder. Distressed that someone had entered her room, Jenn went on to read the note that instructed her a) to hit the play button. When she did, the rock group Pink Floyd told her that she was missed, terribly missed, and that life was an endless circle in a fish bowl. The note then outlined b) an offer to join a Buddha on the roof so that they could at least swim together in this weird world, and that c) her favourite French wine was already uncorked and breathing. She said "Phew" out loud, got into the bikini bottoms, wrapped a towel around her shoulders and went up the stairs.

There was Marty, wearing a bathing suit with pictures of Groucho Marx smoking a cigar on it. There was Marty, with his enormous Buddha.

But that was a long time ago and now she couldn't bear him. She'd e-mailed her father when she first got involved with Marty; her dad told her to have her fun but not get too attached because this Martin fellow belonged to a vast tribe of nomadic losers. Jenn knew her chemistry professor father had to say these things, though she'd already begun to see Marty as an old man who still believed he was twenty-five. He claimed to be a photojournalist but never sent his pictures anywhere. He just wore the camera around his neck as a fashion accessory. He quoted Janis Joplin as if she was an oracle. He never washed before getting into bed. And she was getting very tired of being known as the Buddha's girlfriend.

But, there'd also been that abandoned Mayan girl. The child had hurt her foot badly and her parents had left her at the hospital; they simply couldn't take care of her anymore. Eventually she was brought to the orphanage. Somewhere around seven years old, she'd clung to the fence, crying, until Jenn had to force her to come inside for the night, the girl's skin almost burning in Jenn's arms. The child had torn off her dressing.

And then that night in bed, Marty was shaking, weeping beyond anything Jenn could do for him. It was as if the peasant girl had been his own daughter. One of his tears had managed to fall into one of her eyes, stinging it, making her suddenly fear HIV, but she pushed that thought away, believing she could trust him when he'd insisted at the start that he was clean. The tear stuck with her though, eventually becoming an accusation she held against herself.

She didn't feel Marty's terrible grief. Christ, the place was an orphanage, she told herself. All of the children had been dumped here. Outrage, flickers of slow, light sadness, even anger at the children—these were all familiar emotions, but she could never summon the anguish that had overtaken Marty.

Jenn didn't judge herself for this seeming insensitivity, but she could wonder about it. What was happening to her? She felt a mixture of respect and envy for Marty that night, though later, as the weeks passed, she just felt more estranged—from him, from other people. How could she make this whole mess cohere?

When Jenn continuously told her Canadian friend Fran that she'd been unable to find the time to take notes to begin the book he wanted her to write, she'd been lying. Everything needed to become more private, so she burrowed and burrowed into herself, confiding little to anyone. She kept a notebook—part diary, part scrapbook, address book, but mostly a place to hide things. She found herself retreating more and more often into its pages. She'd been working on it in the Spanish school when she'd heard some students going over their visit to the orphanage the previous day. Listening to them, she wrote:

As I write, I hear the Spanish students next door. Each student has his/her individual tutor and is describing the orphanage, now that they're authorities on the matter. One just spoke about the situation of the parents—they exist but don't want to care for their children for "rasones differentes." I'd told them that when I spoke about the new girl and I shouldn't have. For crying out loud! That little girl waiting in vain for her parents to return—her fucking torment, her isolation—is now being made into an exercise in a Spanish lesson. Tell me about what you saw, the teacher says, use as many new words as you can.

This is obscene. I will never, never do that to her. I won't even talk about her. No one will ever learn about that child from me.

I don't know what to do.

Stay here for years, make this my work, or go back home and earn some real money to do some more travelling?

What I'd really like to do is walk back to Canada. But who could I do it with? The very first thing I have to do is to leave Marty; I can't have him trailing around me for the rest of my life. He won't admit it, but what he's looking for is a woman to support him.

Why do I always end up with weird men? Why can't I ever figure out what I need to do?

She had no idea there were so many ways of being alone. It seemed that with each week another different incarnation of loneliness presented itself to her. One such demon even urged her to take a knife and carve the long lines of Guatemala down her skin, but noticing that she was getting fatter under her upper arms was enough to bring her back to the mundane, deny herself the comfort of what she knew was just self-pity.

Working in the garden helped, merely squatting on its terraced, far too lumpy earth made things better, except that she'd started the project with John, and he was in Mexico with Ashley. At least John was actually doing something with his life. Being with the Buddha was an excuse, a fretful laziness that she must never allow herself to repeat. So, she would let him go with her to Guatemala City, permit him to wander with her for a week through parts of the country she hadn't yet seen. She knew that it would sicken her, and that she would always regret wasting her final week in Guatemala that way, but she hoped that this punishment would imprint itself so deeply that she would never allow herself to get into this kind of situation again. At least the kids would have the garden, its fresh, clean vegetables; that would be the only thing she would leave of herself in Xela.

Marty had been receiving letters from his lawyer saying he absolutely had to return to the States. Pronto, the lawyer said, pronto, pronto, pronto. He'd asked her to go back with him, create a spectacle, get married, and raise more Buddhas, something which even he knew was absurd. She ran her fingers over his face, and then tussled him awake, told him he could go with her as far as the airport. They'd have a last week together.

She shared his can of cream soda on the bus, and tried to fall asleep, licking her teeth to dissolve the pop's plastic stickiness. Every so often the bus would pause in places she'd never see again, jostle through pockets of village noise that woke her, only to be reminded of Marty's beard on the top of her head. His Buddha was hidden underneath his favourite shirt. She'd tied her rust-coloured bandana over her hair, and she could feel his breath through the cotton. It was as bad as hers was.

From above, she dreamed she was floating like the dawn, with its thick haze of Guatemalan light, layers of slow and sightless sun and cloud engulfing the tiny bus making its way on the road that sometimes was hidden by trees.

Jenn woke having to pee badly.

"Penguins," Marty declared when he saw she'd awoken, "I feel as though penguins are rioting, joyously rioting in my brain. Black and white little darlings. I can feel them sliding off my brain and splashing into the Antarctic. Freezing green waves, sure, but it's so much fun. That's how you make me feel Jenny. It's why I love you, you know that, don't you?"

"Do you have any idea where we are?"

"We're here Jenn, we're always here."

"No, I'm serious, do you know where we are?"

"No, but you were grinding your teeth again. I think you should change your mind, come back with me to Oregon. Like I told you,

you'd love the coast. We could go fishing with the pelicans. Go riding on a whale."

"That's what's nice about you Marty, you never give up."

Spending two days in a village en route to Guatemala City, Jenn somehow slips into another self, managing to think with her eyes as she shoots over twenty rolls of film. She frames and focuses without judgment, sometimes shooting rapidly, sometimes not taking a picture in an hour of meandering. Her Spanish has become pretty good. She squats in front of an old Mayan woman in the market and tries speaking to her. After a few moments of silence, Jenn knows that she's invisible to the woman, no, not invisible, she's merely irrelevant. Even though some of the pictures, including one of Marty lagging behind, will be fine enough to eventually mount a show in Saskatoon, the greatest treasure she brings back from her whole time away is this sense of being superfluous.

Can stories go on forever or do they have to end?

One Christmas morning, Jenn will drive north of Winnipeg in a blizzard to visit her family. She's well prepared with a thermos of black coffee, some food, flares, and a couple of blankets. The trunk is crammed with presents. The windshield wipers can't keep up with the snow, so she pulls over and hacks away at the ice. By the time she clears off the windows, she has to start again. Suddenly disturbed by the noise the ice scraper makes, her dog begins to leap around, managing to hit the car's lock mechanism. The keys are still in the ignition.

Heat and music emanate from the car's locked doors.

It matters, it doesn't matter to Jenn as she falls asleep beside the passenger door in the snow; she's reached eighty-one years old.

Fran Saunders is an Ambitious Man

— One Saturday morning a long puddle on the new asphalt driveway held trees, clouds, the neighbours' perpetually gleaming car, and just then, a magpie. The scent of wet evergreen wandered through the air, as did mosquitoes, but the night's rain hadn't reached the sunflower seeds Melissa and her dad had planted much too deeply by the front steps.

From the window, Fran Saunders mouthed a thank-you to his wife, Jackie, for taking Melissa to her gymnastics lesson, but even more he waved to his daughter, who for months had been entranced by the excrement of animals and even dolls, Melissa who was jealous at daycare when anyone else played with her friend Kyle, the little boy whom she claimed she would marry and live with forever at the West Edmonton Mall.

His two women disappeared down the residential street, his wife in sweats driving a little girl who'd insisted that morning on wearing an old birthday tiara and her cream white tutu.

Fran hadn't wanted children, but sometimes they astonished him.

He greatly admired his daughter for her nightmares.

She'd once awoken crying "I can't draw stars," and another night let out the utterly forsaken "leopards are too hard." Fran hadn't been home to hear these dreams because he usually worked nights, but he was proud of his little girl. Deep down, her mind already knew ambition as a thin and accusatory nerve.

He would see to it that this nerve received nurturing.

Tired from his Friday evening shift at Regina's *Daily News*, where he worked night shifts as an editor on the news desk, Fran usually enjoyed his time alone Saturday mornings going through *The World & Dispatch*, comparing how they'd cropped this photo or written up that story. At least *The World & Dispatch* tried for real journalism.

The accountants had taken over most newspapers—no one cared anymore about what delivering the news was for. Glad for the rain, Fran sat on the patio in the backyard, after having wiped off a chair with one of his daughter's shirts from the laundry basket. The sky was still overcast; one small cloud in the distance looked as though it had been forced from an exploding oil tanker that carried raw, boiling mercury.

The people they'd bought their house from had rented it to students. No one had looked after the lawn. Or the flowerbeds. There were dandelions everywhere, but their seeds were marvelously combustible. He found a small pleasure in taking a lighter to a puff of dandelion seeds to watch it flare into a collapsing globe of ash, each immolation contributing to the health of next year's lawn, though he practiced restraint. It would be idiotic to spend an entire morning setting dandelion seeds alight.

Fran knew himself to be an acceptably intelligent, efficient, and disciplined man. However, it was these very qualities that made him suspect that the last seven days resembled those tiny husks of dandelion flame. Each day happened too fast. He was no further ahead this week than he'd been last Saturday. Then as now, he'd found himself flipping through *The World & Dispatch*, getting up occasionally to set some dandelions on fire. Then as now, he'd been pondering how he could change things and start again, begin his real life.

It was true that another week meant a little more money earned for Melissa's education, but you were supposed to use a week to add to your life, not just breeze through the days. A week was for building something. Fran believed he could honestly call himself a journalist at heart. He was better than his job; and he was still pissed off with his supervisor, Edwin, who took him off reporting when Melissa was born and Fran needed to have some kind of regular schedule. Working the desk would be better for everyone, Edwin claimed with that sanctimonious smile of his. Fran didn't mind editing because he liked precision, but he wasn't going anywhere on the night desk.

Working on the news desk was, as one of his younger colleagues put it, "a desk sentence." The rules were utterly simple in this business: the only people who got anywhere were columnists, so Fran had been working out some ideas to start his own column. He planned to write his own for a while, and somehow try to find the time to do some genuine journalism and sell it to a good magazine in the States. Then it would be goodbye editing, maybe even goodbye to the *News*.

The problem was—he first had to come up with something that the *News* would print, but it would also have to be something he could respect. Not an easy combination. Working full-time, raising a daughter, looking after a house; he was having trouble coming up with any satisfactory ideas.

He looked at the past week and only four things had been achieved.

Yesterday, he'd swatted a fly but only stunned it, so he had to crush it with a Kleenex; feeling its tiny skull break between his fingers had been a new sensation.

He'd finally scored a book review, even if it was only about the history of birdwatching in the province.

Because there were still scars from his having fought against having children, it was heartening to receive his wife's approval last Sunday night by entertaining Melissa. It was his job to convince her that hair could be washed without anybody screaming. He'd made her a deal. If there were no tears he'd do some tricks.

While she was getting shampooed he'd taken two identical coffee cups and filled one with shaving cream. After showing her the empty cup, he'd turned off the lights, switched cups, and had Melissa pass her hand over it: abracadabra—snowman poop. The little girl had slapped her hands down into the water with delight, getting water in her mother's eyes.

Coffee grounds became bug poop, and then he'd marched into the bathroom as Mustard Man, a paper towel over his face decorated with mustard eyes, nose, and smile, held in place with an Our Lady Peace promotional toque he'd gotten at work.

Clothespins on his fingers made him a witch.

The fourth thing he'd achieved he was still working on. He'd once heard somewhere that thinking about your life in the third person could help in gaining a necessary sense of perspective. But it was more difficult than he'd imagined.

Francis Saunders was sitting, is sitting, in a backyard with a swing set, and his knees hurt because of arthritis, though he isn't all that old, but doctors don't know squat about immune spiraling diseases. He's only thirty-six. He's married, with one child, and works for a newspaper.

But this isn't good enough—it doesn't really say anything. Start over.

Francis is in okay shape, is a good husband, but he's more than a husband and a father and a newspaperman.

But is that yet true? No, it isn't.

Okay, summed up, Fran has no favourite foods, doesn't have any grey in his hair, and in the morning he always thinks about money. Not in a bad way, because money is abstract. He's in the hole a long, long way, but it doesn't matter because he's making all right money now. Money is, but mostly isn't, important.

Fran has a friend who'd suddenly found himself completely out of money and had panicked, had phoned him to say, "I'm down to $200," and Fran had told Jackie that it was impossible to understand how someone could be surprised by their finances. Fran knows, within a hundred dollars, what each account holds, how much is owed to credit cards, Lisa's parents, all that—$20,000 to them, $7,800 to Visa, $4,100 to the Toronto Dominion Bank for Lisa's student loans, $8,000 his own.

This isn't right, either.

Fran relaxes: this is just an exercise, talking in the third person, thinking in the third person. It doesn't matter—no one can see what he's doing. Fran knows more than anything that nothing matters unless it's done right. He looks at his hands, the round ball that joins his thumb to his hand, and he hates aging, but life, Fran knows, is concrete; he isn't asking anyone for help.

Fran knows his life is happening too fast.

Fran's real problem is that although he can observe things, thought that he'd seen some new trends, when he starts writing all he has are facts, no vision.

It was better when he'd spent time in The Riders' locker room, or had to cover something for city council. But a column had to do more than just let people know the results of a game. But athletes had been so easy to spend time with. And cops, he'd liked cops. You always knew where you stood with cops.

No, a column has to make hundreds of readers, make that thousands of readers, think you are their personal friend. They want to turn to you every week. And sure, some readers would disagree with you, but that was good.

The important thing is to intellectually participate in the life of your times.

But figuring out your own times wasn't easy.

Earlier that morning Fran had driven by an abandoned grocery cart on Wascana Parkway. That made sense enough, but there was a pink flamingo in the cart. Then he'd stopped at a traffic light only to see a woman holding a full glass of water and brushing her teeth in the car beside him. Both the flamingo and the woman were absurd, and yet there they were, impossible to ignore. It must be that there was something about the way people were living now that escaped him.

Fran had been fingering his long and purposefully unkempt mustache when the sounds of kids skateboarding interrupted his efforts at narrating himself into perspective. A bunch of them had discovered the freshly paved, gorgeously smooth driveway. He got up and told them pleasantly to bugger off because he'd worked all night and had to go to sleep. They were disappointed, but left without a fuss. He saw a towering cluster of dandelions on the front lawn and began setting them alight when a couple walked by.

There was nothing in the young man's eyes, but she was crying. She's afraid to go home and face her parents, Fran realized. He approached the couple, and noticed the girl was biting a candy necklace. The young man unlocked the passenger door of the car parked on the street, lit a cigarette, took a drag, glared at Fran, and then flicked the cigarette into a puddle on the road. When they drove away, the girl turned to look back at the house they'd just left. Then they were gone. Someone lost her virginity last night, Fran concluded, glad that his daughter wasn't a teenager yet.

Jackie had told Fran about the all-night party when he'd come home from work. It had been so loud that she'd wanted to phone the police, but what could you do? The Pedersons were friends and if their son—not a bad kid really—had had some friends over when his parents were off to Saskatoon, well, you couldn't really call the cops down on him.

Fran took the junk mail inside and went downstairs to check his e-mail before going to bed. There was a message from Jenn, a woman who'd once interned for a few weeks at the paper. She'd grown disillusioned with journalism, believing it only told people what they already knew, and was now working at an orphanage somewhere in Latin America. Once again, Fran encouraged her to write a feature article about her experiences and send it to him; somehow he'd convince the *News* to publish it. Every now and then they'd print a piece about someone local doing something unusual. She was depressed about her working conditions, and herself, so Fran wrote back that her life would become her own when, and only when two things happened: she had to fail at something she really wanted to do; and she had to succeed at something that she considered to be utterly important.

Only a few hours later, his daughter was shaking him. "Wake up sleepybed, you promised me you'd take me to Robin's house, you promised." The tiara and ballet outfit were gone; Melissa was in shorts and a Sponge Bob Square Pants T-shirt. And her nails were sparkling pink. Jackie must have done them when he was sleeping.

And indeed he had promised to take Melissa to Robin's house. Robin was Melissa's age, the daughter of his oldest friend, Cory, whom he'd met in public school. As soon as he was awake, they'd go and visit Cory and his youngest daughter.

"Coffee first, you know Daddy needs coffee before he can get going."

"Sleepybed," he said to himself going downstairs to check his e-mail. It was going to be sad when she lost those unique words of hers; already the two-year-old's "utties" had become the four-year-old's elephants. Maybe *The World & Dispatch* had replied to an idea for a feature he'd sent to them earlier that morning explaining why Saskatchewan couldn't be compared to any other province.

Cory had taken up brewing his own beer, but you had to drink more than one, because Cory had a very thin skin. His beer was a king among beers. Much better than anything you could buy. This thin skin of Cory's had served him well; whatever game Cory played, Cory won.

This was why Fran had remained friends with the man; Cory had an edge that Fran lacked, and Fran thought that if he watched Cory long enough he would eventually catch up and then leave his buddy breathing dust. Someone else might call Cory a bully, but to Fran he was simply ruthless, a quality he greatly admired.

The other kids had corralled them together some twenty-five years ago. Fran had been sick the day before and so missed when the new boy had been introduced to the grade four class. Up until then, Fran had more or less ruled his peers, and the other kids, especially the girls. Fran would recognize much later, it was the girls who really, really wanted to see this new big-headed kid put in place.

The young Cory had accepted that this contest was simply part of the natural order of things; and Fran saw that this Cory guy was going to relish the fight regardless of the result. After some initial shoves, and realizing the other boy's strength, Fran raised his hand, not in a grown-up handshake, but as one warrior greets another. Within seconds, he was on his knees, and his fingers felt broken.

As teenagers, they'd sometimes go to somebody's parents' cabin during March break. It was always Cory who scored with a girl, and then was up at dawn insisting that anyone who didn't chug down a beer was a candy-ass. Ditto if you didn't join him rolling around naked in the snow.

And it was Cory who fell for Fran's sister.

They'd once had a party and his sister had curled up in somebody else's lap. There'd been a brawl that Cory easily won. The only time that Cory had ever obeyed Fran was when he told him that night that he had to clean up the blood on the cement porch before their parents came home. Cory used beer and Comet and then washed the mess away with piss. The stains lasted for years.

But now, Cory had fashionably shaven his head and sold drugs for a pharmaceutical company. But he still listened to the music he'd enjoyed as a teenager. Because his wife was a periodontal surgeon, Cory lived in a house that was a kingdom of fine wood and enormous windows. Every moment of the day some part of the house glowed with sunlight over a wealth of plants they hired a company to oversee. The kitchen alone was larger than Fran's living room. The upstairs architecture seemed Japanese to Fran, though he doubted whether Cory recognized it as such.

Fran won the first game of pool in Cory's game room, but lost the next two. Cory travelled a lot for his job, and as he leaned over the table, sinking ball after ball, he told Fran about the nurse he'd been seeing in Saskatoon. It sometimes disturbed Fran that he'd slept with only three women; Cory had had more women than that by the time he was sixteen. Feeling punchy, Fran told his friend that he was a great guy but he lacked ambition. He should've become a MD instead of a drug pusher. Hell, he could at least have become a pharmacist. It was fun to see the liquid fury in Cory's eyes.

"But honey," Cory spat back, "I done did marry rich ass instead. Seems to me you're still slaving the night shift."

The two men were interrupted by Melissa who, as usual, was overwhelmed by the havoc, the sheer abundance of Robin's toys. This time it was the new dollhouse, and that was enough for Fran. He announced that it was time to get ready to leave.

"Sweetie," he whispered to his daughter who still wanted to play, "get ready, we're going to Toys"R"Us. We'll get you the best dollhouse in the world."

There wasn't much traffic, but they had to hurry because it was almost six o'clock and the store would soon be closing. Fran kept getting red lights. He kept up a steady chatter with his daughter, telling her to let him know when she saw the sign for the toy store.

He wondered if he could write a column on making homemade beer or wine, or perhaps he could do something on what happened to the members of his high school class from Campbell. Cory could never do anything like that. He tried squashing that thought, competing with Cory was beneath him, but deep down he knew that the desire to have people respect him would never go away.

Zipping through an amber light, Fran saw a police car's lights open up behind him in the mirror.

It so happened that the cop wouldn't accept his explanation, even with Melissa crying in the back seat. Thank God she hadn't undone the seatbelt like she sometimes did. Damn Edwin for taking him off reporting. Back then, he probably would have known this guy. But to this cop, young and eager, he was just some guy that deserved to be pulled over.

And then the cop wanted to know if Fran had been drinking.

Minutes later, Fran had to endure waiting as the cop radioed the police station, so that somebody could phone Jackie to call a cab so she could pick up Melissa while he got a trip downtown so formal impaired charges could be made. Sitting in the back behind the grill, sunk in the heavy, deep, absurdly comfortable seat of the cruiser, Fran watched the girls disappear in a taxi. The cop kept talking on the radio. As the tow truck arrived to haul away his car, Fran knew that his life was over.

But, in this, as with a number of other things, he was mistaken.

Angels

— Angels, the good ones that is, love suddenly released odours, paper of all kinds, and water; the more difficult are drawn to stone, the noiseless laughter caught by the deaf, forensics. They frequently cluster like clouds of steam in bathrooms. One hundred and nine dropped in one morning while Leah lay soaking in a tub, the shower curtain pulled tight, sealing her into an enclave she'd first created in childhood. Sunlight poured through the bathroom's frosted window, and when she narrowed her eyelids, the black and white swans on the curtain drifted in a gorgeous haze of plastic. This was the first of three days off from the nursing home where she worked mostly nights as an aide. Away from soiled bodies, and brains that had been blasted into bloody confetti, she treated herself to rose musk bath beads, the radio, and her favourite Mexican beer.

This is the happiest story I know.

Isn't it impossible not to love certain things? Having a few days off. The feel of the random world.

Time, with nothing happening inside it.

Celebrating a week of dead rock stars, the radio station began its Roy Orbison tribute. Leah was iffy about old music, despite her father's having once tried to convince her that no one, absolutely no one, could touch Orbison's voice when he found the right song. He'd played one track after another when she was a teenager, trying to make his point, when she'd suggested John Lennon as a rival. Okay, okay, you got me there, he'd said, openly pleased that she'd joined his game, but insisting that those two were in a class of their own.

That morning she'd walked home from work. After drinking a coffee beside the fountain in front of the nursing home, she'd taken the shortcut along the highway and discovered the head of a magpie. Its eyes were still open, and dust hadn't settled on it yet; its head was a gleam of black and green and blue. Another time she'd found a wallet stuffed with calling cards from the city's numerous escort services. It'd been the dog's ear though, that had startled her into keeping track of what lay on the roadside. Usually a week would go by before anything different joined the day-glow straws, pine cones, junk food wrappers and broken beer bottles, their dark amber shards scattered amongst worn tire tracks and impoverished dandelions. She'd been thinking about Denise, the patient she'd liked best, a woman who'd long ago fallen deeply away from her surroundings, when she'd noticed the bird's head exposed in the dusty grass, impossible to miss. Because of the angels, she couldn't tell anymore whether what she saw was supposed to be there, an accident, or if things had been arranged especially for her.

Like all of us, Leah had known about angels since childhood. But in the flesh, they were so much different from what she'd imagined. Translucent, yes, and when she saw them she felt a warm light glowing beneath her skin. But strangely, they always made her think about water. All kinds of water. Water from a tap, by sand, rain. What kept her on her toes, though, was their quixotic intelligence. This grew to worry her. As Leah well knew, intelligence is often preternaturally at home in chaos.

The angels had first revealed themselves earlier that summer at the fountain by the nursing home, its austerity, she learned later, a relief from centuries of European grandeur. A dozen or so streams of water cascaded into a cement pool freshly painted turquoise. The wind had been making a loose gauze of mist, and she'd been idly staring through it into the shrubbery in the distance, when the spray suddenly broke up into separate water droplets, each tumbling and refracting light. Inch-long aqua damselflies floated above the gravel sidewalk, seeking mosquitoes. In between the droplets a jumbled baroque of hands waved, and she felt as though she'd suddenly woken up to find herself rocking at the top of a Ferris wheel, surprisingly unafraid because heights usually made her panic.

But what overwhelmed her most was the unfamiliar sensation of being seen. Not in the sense of surveillance, but something more generous. She'd never felt less alone; the angels were paying a unique kind of attention to her.

Soon her visitors began to show up in other places, at home, when she bathed the men and women at work. She'd straightaway discovered that angels are Dadaists at heart. On one occasion, she'd gone out for a newspaper to show them what a headline was—angels don't read very much—and when she came back, the numbers from her alarm clock were missing. She didn't find them until she made dinner.

Angels, she discovered, are obsessed with details, but they have no sense of scale. While it's true that their silliness can flicker into a fierce strangeness, often they simply want to play. A little while after their first meeting, they'd asked Leah what she thought of the word "frazil." It's an interesting word, one angel had said. Because she'd never heard of it before, they'd spelled it out—f-r-a-z-i-l. When they went at its meaning, however, they explained it metaphysically, going slowly, so she couldn't help but understand.

"Look," she'd said, always careful to check their obsessions, "aren't there other things to talk about?"

—*Okay*, one said, *no metaphysics.*

—*But everything's metaphysical*, another claimed.

—*How about what happens when somebody's boyfriend wants to lose his virginity in a car on a side road in the middle of an afternoon snowstorm?*

Angels, Leah quickly learned, are surprisingly earthy. Like us, they're intrigued by sex, and like us, they're not sure how to understand it.

—*What about pearl necklaces on nude women sunbathing in Greece?*

—*No*, replied another, *let's talk about the blurred cemeteries of the heart.*

Only rarely did Leah lose her patience with the angels.

"But we've already gone over all of that," Leah said; though this wasn't entirely fair, they'd never mentioned pearl necklaces before.

—*Tell us about it, everything new is under the sun,*" they'd said, laughing, this time in a chorus, a rarity, since angels almost never agree with each other.

The art of conversation is lost on angels. When do they really mean what they say? How can you tell when they're just screwing around from when they're hiding in parables?

—*Quick*, one of them had said on their initial visitation, *somebody dropped something over there in the grass.*

And it was true, there was an object in the grass—even though Leah was a continent away from any ocean, there it was, a stingray, motionless in a block of ice, imperial, a stranger to the prairie with its whiff of wet salt.

—*A banner day*, another angel offered in a hopeful voice.

"Am I losing my mind," Leah wondered that first time by the fountain.

—*How should we know?* they'd said, *we're angels.*

As she scrubbed beneath her nails, added some more hot water, the light in the bathroom window began to waver. Over time, she'd learnt that changes in light meant the angels were arriving, often passing through her oldest and most worn memories to greet her. She looked up to see an image of her father as a young man. He was turning on a lamp.

Once upon a time Leah's father had given her that very lamp for her birthday, and it still watched over her on a night table. Its emerald-coloured stem stood on a plastic base that was supposed to remind you of marble. When she'd had childhood nightmares, her father used to come into her bedroom, turn on the lamp, and read a story. He read her all kinds of stories, from the standard Brothers Grimm to *The How and Why Wonder Book* about dinosaurs. Her father had been a high school geography teacher, so dinosaurs made more sense to him than fairy tales.

"Do you want to know how big a brontosaurus was," he'd ask, and flicker the lamp while making weird noises, trying hard to help her imagine a dinosaur walking across a swamp, a swamp in the Jurassic period to be precise. "Well sweetheart," he'd say, "let's put it this way, a stegosaurus would be about the size of Mommy's car. A bronto, well, you'd have to line up two transport trucks just to get the picture."

Leah loved every page, each sound her dad would make, and every dinosaur battle that took place on the covers. A white pillow would become a cloud for swooping pterodactyls, scrunched up blankets would provide an arena for the classic showdown between the lumbering evil of a T. Rex and the gentle, but never-say-die courage belonging to a triceratops. A single child, it had taken Leah years to learn that dinosaurs weren't her own personal property.

But nothing disturbed her father more than being alone, and this was a serious dilemma because Leah's mother worked nights as an industrial nurse. The emerald lamp was rarely turned off at night and it had seen Leah and her father curled up together after countless stories, both of them waiting for the car to pull into the carport, the sound of a voice. While the family would eat breakfast, they'd talk about patients while an endless series of white uniforms went through the wash. Her dad would go off to school, where his students, contour maps, and slides of volcanoes awaited him.

She'd sit beside him at night while he marked, working on a drawing of the muddy hailstorm that hit Pompeii when Vesuvius erupted, a catastrophe that offended her father's sense of order. How could such a thing happen? They were kings, he'd say, the Romans were kings. They knew more about the world than we'll ever know. They didn't deserve Vesuvius.

"Why doesn't your mother ever come home?" he'd ask, not really to his daughter, but to what to him was mostly an empty room, and as he sharpened his pencil, she'd sharpen hers as well.

In retrospect, Leah sympathized with her father—he had a mind that could do just about anything, but it was a mind that bordered on chaos. He shouldn't have taught geography. His true bent was metaphysics, just like the angels.

This morning in the bath, the angels made her remember him from out of the blue, this time almost fully; she could see the two of them spinning around the living room to "Pretty Woman," a heavy child cozying up next to a jaw that smelled of Old Spice.

"Tell me something I don't know about my Dad."

—*Why not that bit about Hitler and Speer?* one angel asked another.

"Go on," Leah said.

—*Practically every man of your father's generation is fascinated by the Second World War—remember the constant documentaries, the war movies? You can check up on this. Look into your father's copy of Albert Speer's* Inside the Third Reich, *and you'll find the book cracks opens to a photograph of Hitler and Speer at Hitler's private house in the mountains, going for a walk in the snow, each, as Speer says, dwelling on his own thoughts.*

—*Your father couldn't get away from that picture.*

—*He used to just sit there, thinking: "two architects taking a break from it all."*

Some years later, shortly after her father's death, Leah will carefully cut the photo from the book and frame it, but this morning in the bathtub the story is just a slight oddity from her father's life. No one today but the angels knows, though, about the guest who, sitting by the cactus for hours trying to drum up the courage to steal one of Hitler's pens, ended up being reprimanded instead for falling asleep during one of the *Fuehrer's* interminable movies.

This is a happy story, the happiest I know; but it's hard to keep it in one place.

Angels push people not necessarily into virtue, or away from danger, but drag them along into the kinks on the surface of things. And though Leah was a match for them in some ways, she didn't understand the complexities of their multiple fascinations.

—*A disguised soldier is found out because Japanese and Korean people wash their faces differently,* another angel interjected.

—Why must you keep talking about that?

—It's perfect, don't you see? The world in a grain of sand.

"I want you to do something," Leah said.

—Anything for you sweetheart.

—Well, not anything, we're not magicians you know.

"I want to know what it feels like to be somebody else."

—Are you sure?

"I'm twenty. I already know me, let me find out what it's like to be somebody else."

—That we can do.

—Easy as pie.

"I don't want to go up there," a woman about Leah's age was telling her but Leah wasn't herself; the angels had placed her inside a man's body. Leah recognized that they were at the university, standing beneath an old Volkswagen on top of a pylon riveted to a small hill, someone's idea of sculpture. It was a perfect place to hide away and party. Leah had once smoked weed up in the Volkswagen with her boyfriend Anthony.

What's going on here? Leah wondered, but the question made no impression on whoever was climbing up the ladder into the belly of the car. Careful not to crack the bottle of wine he was carrying, he pushed open a trapdoor and looked down.

"You said you wanted to talk, we'll talk here."

The man sat behind the steering wheel, and turning to face the woman, asked whether she wanted a drink. A glance showed Leah that the woman was a goth—torn fishnets, high leather boots, black widows for earrings. Utterly red lips.

"Cabernet Sauvignon. The medical establishment says it's a cure for everything that ails you."

At this, the woman became incoherent. Leaping from fear to accusations to woe, she couldn't keep still. Leah felt the man's disgust and curiosity as he removed his hand from the woman's, and leaned against the door, safely welded shut.

"You asshole," she said over and over, her cries amplified within the car's interior, which gave off the aroma of old marijuana, sweat.

Invisible, remote, Leah was surprised that another person's mind corresponded so closely to her own. Thinking was the same, mechanically at least. What disturbed her was the peculiar, almost physical, mood saturating this man—she'd never imagined such a sensation, its appalling specificity. This can't be the way all men perceive the world, Leah thought, this man is a monster.

He'd knowingly infected this woman with herpes—this much Leah could easily discern. His skin was lordly, tightly paranoid, each fingernail sent distinct messages to his brain, made a kind of emotional noise. When he moved his hand, or tilted the bottle to his thickening mouth, shifted in his clothes, the physical impression was not even vaguely familiar.

"What am I going to do, I've got an exam tomorrow," the woman wept.

"So what."

"But school's the only thing I have now, it's all I can count on, you asshole."

"Oh come on. Stop this bullshit Kath."

"Are you still sleeping with people?"

"Why not? Somebody gave it to me."

"You can't do that."

"Just watch. Let you in on a secret? People always get what they want."

"I can't believe this. You're my second. I've only fucked two guys, and I end up with you, I just can't believe this. What am I supposed to do?"

From the moment she'd left a message on his answering machine that ended with "See you later, Alligator," he'd despised her—the intolerable, eternal smugness of women in love.

"Tell me exactly what the doctor told you," the man instructed. "Let me hear every single word."

He was going to enjoy this immensely. Even more exhilarating—

there was something he wasn't telling her. He'd tested positive for HIV.

"Did they do a blood test?" he wanted to know.

"I've got to get out of here," Leah thought.

The DJ introduced another Orbison number, and Leah instantly lost what the angels had shown her, except for a momentary sting, which felt like a pellet had struck her cheek. Or that a child had pinched her. She splashed water on her skin, then soothed it with Dove.

Various kinds of soap crowded the ledge of the bathtub, each to be used on a different part of her body.

—*The windowless monad,* one angel observed.
—*I hate it when they ask questions like that.*
—*Like what?*
—*What am I supposed to do?*
—*Time flies.*
—*How could it?*
—*Just look.*

As everyone knows, angels have difficulty coming to grips with time, but boy-o-boy does it intrigue them. To us, time is an hour being skinned slowly, or a quicksilver flash, too swift to register, but to angels, time is plastic, ubiquitous, a pearly ice cube in a glass of Coke. Leibnitz, the angels knew, had almost got it right. Leah in her bath, the conversation in the Volkswagen, Hitler and Speer—each took place in the same unleavened instant, and yet, each utters its various eternities. If angels could wear tattoos, instead of a woman's name, their upper arms would be emblazoned with one fiery word: ALREADY.

—*But that's the beauty of it—time flies,* one angel said, physically close to Leah, but far beyond her hearing. *Time's like a mosquito buzzing in a jar, a mosquito, mind you, that was only just plucked from a railroad track and then plunked in a jar.*
—*Too Victorian.*

—Pear's soap was made for a queen.

—Tender nights?

—The colour's wrong.

—She's shaving her legs. I love it when she shaves her legs.

—Incredible texture, shaving cream, don't you think?

—Her old boyfriend would enjoy seeing this. He's been thinking about her for months.

—Mercy!

—What should she do?

—I think she should gather her inner resources.

—Oh no you don't. Don't frighten her.

—No one's going to frighten anyone.

—I hate it when you do things like this.

—Like what?

As the bathtub vanished from Leah's sight, she could somehow smell diesel fumes. They'd never pulled a stunt like this one before. She lay with one leg up in the air in the Zen gardens at Kyoto, a pink plastic razor in her hand, and not once in five hundred years has the sand ever been disturbed, except by the monks raking sand, patiently turning the sand into water around rocks that are supposed to remind you of water.

The tourists reached for their cameras.

—You're not going to leave her like that.

—Of course not.

—A nice, suspenseful place, these gardens.

—Put her back.

—Already done.

Leah closed her eyes and then she was back in her bathtub, but it felt gritty. It could only be what it was: sand. She hadn't felt sand in a bathtub since she'd been a child and had come home from the beach. No one in Kyoto believed what they'd seen, except one fellow, who was thrilled that he'd come equipped with a Polaroid camera. The picture developed in front of his eyes—rocks, sand, and a plastic razor, frozen in the air.

The monks hurried to their rakes, the sky threatening everyone with rain.

The second that Leah disappeared, the shower curtain was transformed; instead of the swans, it showed a woman's lower legs in an ancient bathtub, the water an exquisite mirror, a scalpel that cut between worlds. Urchins floated adjacent to a volcano pushing a skyscraper out through its fiery crater, a submerged woman was pinioned to the drain. A bird stiffened on top of a weather-smoothed tree, its creator's life's agony that she couldn't have children.

—*When she was young, she got into a traffic accident. An iron railing entered her hip, exited through her vagina, tearing the labia.*
—*Frida, Frida.*
—*Does anyone really know how to touch her?*
—*Regret's slow alchemy.*
—*Why do women?*
—*Yes.*

When Leah returned from Kyoto, the image wrapped itself around her, and then was gone.

She didn't get to see it; angels always offer more than they give. What, then, are angels for? They begin so tenderly, but once they get going, it's hard for them to stop their anarchic, wasteful nature from taking over.

Leah had once asked them what purpose they served, but they didn't know for certain. They suspect that they're a catalyst that causes forgetting. When she'd told them that that didn't make sense, they simply shrugged their shoulders. But they're wrong about the layers and layers of amnesia. Angels have nothing to do with memory. Unlike us, angels are simply a terrible kind of elaboration.

The beer gone, her body flushed, but free of work's unpleasantness, Leah asked the angels whether they'd gotten what they'd wanted. You never know, they told her. She brushed, then flossed her teeth, gave a brief thought to Kurt Cobain, the newspaper photo of his blood-stained guitar when it had been put up for auction. The radio station would feature his music tomorrow, but tomorrow she'd be sleeping in, probably with Anthony, and why was it that being whisked away from what should have been a solitary bath made her feel so damned cheerful?

She trimmed her pubic hair once more, then turned on the shower to wash away the sand, checked to make sure the apartment door was locked, shut the bedroom blinds, and read a bit by the emerald lamp. She wasn't interested in trying to vary a man's sexual tastes, couldn't change that old people like Denise deteriorated or that angels continued to tear through time to visit her.

For a little more than a half-hour Leah had been, like all of us, a template—the beauty of which no one, least of all the angels, can identify. In a little while she will awake from a nightmare in which a woman who looks like a vampire in fishnet stockings, will repeat "Leah, Leah, you have to find me and tell me I need to be tested for AIDS." But for now, there's the lovely stretching diagonally across cool sheets in the music-less present.

—*I love that vein she has by her eyelid.*
—*Never seen one quite like it myself.*
—*Sunlight is so beautiful on skin.*
—*The taste of cantaloupe.*
—*Such feelings, such feelings inside.*
—*What are pearls going for these days?*
—*Beg your pardon.*
—*You heard me.*

Giraffes

— It wasn't rain that was falling, but hoarfrost, melting off the trees. Bits of ice shaped like branches crunched beneath Bonnie's feet as she walked home on what would become an impossible day. A trio of red-breasted nuthatches watched her. She loved their bright striped faces and their sudden upside-down spiral along the trees. They seemed to concentrate on her before zeroing off through invisible tunnels of airy space that would lead to food.

Regina is in a flyway; for weeks, numerous species stop in the city, many of them on their way south.

It was a Saturday in November, though warm for Regina. A late Indian summer had stalled winter's advance. Last week she'd taken the kids out for Halloween, and it had been the first Halloween in years that children hadn't had to wear winter coats. It was a minor thing, but she recognized that going down the street today, simply making her way home from the bakery, felt different than when she walked down the same sidewalk on Halloween, stopping at each house. She wondered what it would be like to walk on this street when she was old.

On Halloween, Bonnie and her children had knocked at every door except for one. Inge had left her lights off. Clearly her next-door neighbour hadn't wanted visitors that night; she rarely did. It had been Bonnie's two-year-old son's first time trick-or-treating, Jack had chosen the firefighter costume himself, and her daughter had decided to be a ballerina who was also an alligator. Ballet slippers, a pink tutu, and a dragging tail—the five-year-old shared Bonnie's own delight in the ridiculous. Because her daughter was allergic to peanuts, Bonnie had gone around the day before, giving her neighbours bags of potato chips or little toys to give Petra, named after a childhood friend who still lived in Vancouver, Petra who'd recently taken up with a mime artist. A female mime artist. Bonnie could still hear her mother's oddly gratified voice on the phone as she'd delivered this scandalous news from home.

But up ahead that afternoon there were no mimes, only Inge standing with her dog, both stopped in their tracks. Bonnie's diagnosis was bipolar depression. Perhaps the sky was wrong for her elderly neighbour, the day ajar. During these episodes, Inge's head would loosely bob around, a jack-in-the-box ejected from where it usually lived. Bonnie tried coaxing her out with a greeting but Inge ignored her, jerking the leash when Bonnie had reached down to pat Plischi, and then tramping away. That Bonnie's compassion was unnoticed became unimportant to Bonnie; after that Saturday had passed, after what happened, she would never speak to Inge again.

Walking across her lawn, Bonnie picked up a pine cone to take inside; her son believed that they were eggs laid by porcupines.

Ever since the attacks on the World Trade Center in September, Bonnie had tried to revel more deeply in her family. It was hard to find enough time—both she and her husband Rick were doctors. That morning she and the kids had once again visited the Royal Saskatchewan Museum, though they called it the 'Dino House.' There'd been the usual struggle in the gift shop—Rick had spoiled them—but she'd managed to distract the kids by getting them to sign a large get-well card for Megamunch, the museum's T. Rex who was getting his voice box repaired. Covered up with a checkered blanket on the homemade card, a thermometer in his mouth, the dinosaur was obviously in pain. Blue crayoned tears fell from his right eye, making a puddle on the floor. Already dozens of children had expressed their concern, and Bonnie felt her heart spin as her son made his swirl on the big page. She stopped him before he'd made the other names illegible, including his sister's, with its backward R.

The kids had just been put down for their afternoon nap when she returned. Rick was watching CNN—he'd become a newshound that autumn—so she told him about how the war in Afghanistan had entered their neighbourhood that day. Red, white, and blue ribbons had appeared that morning on the corner house. The woman who lived there, Eveline, was unusually generous with her holiday decorations. Thanksgiving scarecrows had been replaced with a coterie of witches, jack-o'-lanterns, two life size vampires; now a long-robed and expensive Santa Claus, a troop of elves, several wreathes, and the Magi drew attention to the house. A good citizen, Eveline had banded her trees to kill the canker worms that infested the city but unlike the rest of the street, she'd also added the tricolour ribbons. Their neatly tied bows hadn't merely been wrapped around the trunks, but had been heavily stapled to the trees so their gesture wouldn't be subjected to the weather. Other people would put up the red, white and blue in the following days, but without Eveline's sense of perfection; unstapled, their ribbons would lose their luster and fray in the coming months. From the couch, Rick announced that Bush had got the Taliban on the run, then thanked her for the cheesecake she'd gotten as a treat from the plaza.

Bonnie hadn't figured out this war yet, so she wrote out a cheque to a charity that involved some doctors she'd met who had already done some work in Afghanistan. After eating the cheesecake, she sat with Rick on the couch and took his hand to cup her pubis. Her period would arrive Tuesday, and its nearness always made her especially horny. So did chocolate, but she knew that aphrodisiacs were myths. As he stroked her through her panties, she glanced at the framed Sunday *Toronto Star* article that commemorated John Lennon's death. The date on the slightly yellowed newspaper was December fourteenth, 1980, years before she'd met her husband. Bonnie didn't like the newspaper page with its enormous picture of Lennon in their living room, but it had been a gift from Rick's dad, and it had followed them through the dozen apartments they'd lived in before finally buying the house.

Neither of them was on call that day, which didn't happen very often, and the kids would sleep another hour at least, so Bonnie whispered, "strawberries and cream," a marital code that still worked. Rick showered quickly. What she liked best were his fingers on her clitoris after he'd cum inside her, his fingertips then were exact and warm, slippery and necessary human silk. Rick had been eager to join her spread out on her stomach on the bed because he'd been up all night working. A sleepless night made him as randy as the dawn, a physiological fact that neither of their medical degrees could explain, but it was always true. He playfully spanked her with Seneca's *Letters From a Stoic*, that week's bedside reading material, before settling in. Every so often Bonnie thought about how utterly appalled lay people would be if they knew how little medicine actually understood about how the body worked. Later, lying on her back and drifting, she suddenly said, *but I'm Jewish*, which wasn't true, but because she said it aloud, her husband leaned over from his thick descent into sleep. Just dreaming I guess, she told him; actually it'd been something she'd once said to Inge.

After an hour, the alarm clock went off. Afternoon sun made the Japanese erotic prints in Bonnie and Rick's bedroom alive with light. Because Rick was taking her out for her birthday dinner at the Cathedral Village Free House that evening, she didn't have time to stay in bed.

Fortunately, the kids were still sleeping, so she had time for a bath. In the mirror, her daily two-kilometre runs looked good on her. She'd bought a new dress and shoes and had found some elbow-length gloves at the thrift shop. Black with sequins, without fingers, perfect. It took her some time to find her toothbrush as it was lost in the mess of bath toys, hairsprays and gels, a dog biscuit, various tubes of toothpaste—everyone had their own flavour, except Petra who would only use baking soda. The hair dryer would waken Jack, so she began to paint her fingernails. Halfway through, Jack began to call for her.

With his thick, sleepy smell clinging to her, she changed him. He held his T. Rex, though it was really a replica of an allosaurus. When he grew up he was going to be a firefighter on a spaceship, a spaceman firefighter who saved dinosaurs. As usual, he told her he had a big dick, something his dad had told him, and she wondered if the girl he'd eventually entice into this exact room was a baby now, or perhaps she wasn't even born yet. Would they get along? Jack certainly hadn't been circumcised. What STDs would be on the loose then? With those blond curls and smile he was going to be a lady's man. Go get Petra up, and then we'll all jump on Daddy. Because she didn't usually wear nail polish, Jack pointed out her funny fingers. Go get your sister.

He wanted his car with the sticker on it.

A few months before that Saturday in November, Rick had attended a conference in Toronto. It had been late August and he'd bought Petra a Groovy Girl at the airport, Bonnie some amber earrings. Jack had received a set of presidential vehicles: Air Force One, a limo, a Secret Service car with its sticker insignia, a helicopter. After September eleventh, Bonnie had considered throwing them out—it just felt weird to see them—but didn't because they were only a child's toys.

There are so many unexpected kinds of time.

Shortly after Bonnie had changed Jack's diaper, Rick had been called in to check on one of his patients. He couldn't get out of it. It was unlikely that Bonnie would receive a similar call, which was good because she had to make muffins for the Stop Hungry Children program at Petra's school.

From the kitchen window, she kept an eye on Jack who was content with his construction toys in the sandbox, but Petra was more anxious for adult company. She'd played with the dog for a while, then her brother, and then had been spinning in circles on her stomach on the swing, looking too often into the window seeking yet one more wave.

But the back gate was now open, and Petra wasn't in the yard.

Sheets of white terror swept through Bonnie at the kitchen window who then was outside screaming her daughter's name. With Jack in her arms, shouting at the dog to get back, Bonnie took in the street beyond the gate, but there wasn't anyone in either direction.

She then phoned the police—and emptiness dazed her when for a moment she couldn't remember what Petra had been wearing—and she then left a message for Rick who had the car, poured unacceptably cold milk into a bottle and threw Jack in their stroller built for two. She remembered to take Petra's emergency allergy kit, but forgot her cellphone.

She first hurried to the playground at the French School. It held children, but not Petra. Going the other way three blocks later, she remembered there was another playground at the school, one for the kindergarten that Petra liked, but she couldn't go back—how could she go back when she had so much new ground to cover?

She'd been running with the stroller but had to stop because one of its wheels had become snagged on some loops of cassette tape a teenager had tossed out of a car the night before.

She noticed that the colours of the passing cars looked not brighter exactly, but different than usual, remembered that trauma usually affected sensory perception, and told her thoughts to shut the fuck up. She'd head for the art gallery. Petra had been saying that she wanted to go there some Sunday. Then Bonnie saw a police car in the grocery store plaza. The cruiser was empty so she went inside.

Petra was riding the mechanical horse, and Inge was speaking German. No one understood that she was telling the police officer that little girls needed to have pony rides. When she saw her mother, Petra was ecstatic. Inge let me have one hundred rides, Mommy. Didn't you Inge? One hundred rides, I counted, but I want to go home now, Petra said. Jack wanted to have his own horse ride, but Bonnie had forgotten her purse at home. The cop suggested that they put the stroller in the trunk; she'd give them a ride home. She'd put the siren on for a moment; that would make both kids happy. But before the policewoman had taken Bonnie and the kids home, Bonnie had stood in front of Inge, looked up into the taller woman's face, and said, "Inge, I forbid you to touch either of my children again. I no longer consider you our neighbour."

Bonnie had learned about Inge in increments, usually over the fence between their houses. About how her father, a tailor, had disappeared into the *Wehrmacht*, about her distaste for southern Germans, her suspicions, how her brother had repeatedly done things to her he shouldn't have but was rich now, about her love of tennis. Inge had repeatedly informed Bonnie that she didn't own the house in which she lived. She was merely a tenant, but she insisted that she didn't sleep with Tyler, the real owner, who was usually out of the city because of government work. She'd never married, and had developed a bad cholesterol problem that was very terribly annoying because she loved deli meat, cream cheese, and bacon. A diet of vegetable soup and fish wasn't fit for dogs. Inge still hoped to be a silvery bride, Bonnie would see. They'd been poor as church bugs during the war. Poorer, because bugs didn't need money! She sang in the choir and had many well-to-do friends. Plischi walked with a limp because a horse on Tyler's farm had kicked him. She'd once almost committed suicide, and had shown Bonnie a long white line on her arm, but an evangelist on television had turned mid-oration precisely then and looked right at her and said *don't*. After placing her hand on the screen, joining his, her life had never been the same.

People always talked about the Jews, Inge once snarled; no one knew what it'd been like to live in Germany back then. You were already guilty. Years of living before the accusations stopped, even in the 1960s in Canada being called a fucking Nazi by the head nurse, who would probably never in her days speak to another person like that again. Inge could still see woman's furious face through the window in the slammed door in the hospital where she worked, the glass protected by a reinforcing grid of something threaded inside it.

"But I'm Jewish," Bonnie had said.

"Then you know what I mean," Inge had responded.

After this exchange, Inge had then burrowed into her house for over a week, only to emerge at dusk to whack tennis balls into the huge wooden backdrop that separated their properties. Finally Inge had shown up at the front door with an absurdly ornate red dress for Petra. She'd sewn it herself because every little girl needs a party dress. And to Bonnie's surprise, Petra had been overjoyed with the dress, its lace and trailing cuffs, even its cumbersome length. In her office at work, Bonnie has a photo of the two kids in the tree house looking across at Inge standing on the packed dirt tennis court, her son entranced by the machine that fired tennis balls, Petra in Inge's dress waving. When her mind was faithful, Inge loved to talk, but she would never enter Bonnie's house, though Inge had once served them an indoor picnic.

Rick had been working, so just the three of them had gone. Jack had been a baby and had slept the whole time in his car seat. Bonnie could see how utterly important their visit was to Inge, and she'd been embarrassed when Inge told her how proud she was to have doctors for neighbours. Everyone on the street had been happy, Inge assured Bonnie, everyone had been delighted when they'd moved in. Two doctors, and their young family were exactly what the street needed.

"Tell me about your mother, Inge," Bonnie had asked.

"A hard woman, she was a very hard woman."

"Did you ever go back to visit her?"

"Once I did, in 1972, but my brother was there and he acted like nothing had ever happened. He only came because he wanted to show off his new car. Everyone was so impressed, but not me, I've got his number."

"You're a brave woman, Inge."

"What's brave have to do with it—I'm just Inge."

"Well, you're wonderful with children."

After they'd eaten, heard once more about the cholesterol problem, her brother's stupid pride, Inge had excused herself to prepare her surprise. After several minutes, Inge had invited them into her bedroom. Upon entering the room, Bonnie's immediate response was that Inge's shrine was a scene from a supernatural thriller; entering her sanctuary, they stepped into the serial killer's lair.

Inge had expertly made some wooden steps, painted them blue, and then added some stars. On the top step she'd placed a manger.

The requisite shepherds, animals and magi, purchased in The Dollar Store, were there, but so were candles, mostly white and all lit, and angels, there seemed to be hundreds of candles and angels of various sizes, all turning in waves of desire toward the infant.

Inge had changed into a gown that touched the floor, not white as would be expected, but a glowing orange that reminded Bonnie of the bubbles in Petra's lava lamp. She'd taken off her socks. Having had some experience with birthday parties, Petra merrily began to blow out the candles. Bonnie had been afraid that this would anger Inge, but it hadn't; she'd joined in blowing out the flames, telling them that everyone had to make a secret wish.

Inge had given Petra one of her own dolls that afternoon, but Bonnie wondered whether Inge's bedroom would give Petra nightmares.

Recently Petra had begun startling Bonnie with a hesitant yet heartfelt theology. For some reason, Petra's revelations took place almost always in the bathtub. Bonnie bathed with the kids. Petra would lie back amidst her mother and brother's slippery legs and inform Bonnie that God is bigger than anything. When I die I'll become an angel. One night Petra had improvised a little song that proclaimed God was Love and that he was making toys for children and that he ate germ bugs. God loves little girls more than little boys she'd let everybody know. At this, Bonnie realized that Petra wasn't getting these things from friends at school. Inge. Bonnie had been forced to have a little talk with her neighbour; she'd instructed Inge never, never again to speak to Petra, or Jack, about religion.

When I die, I'll become an angel.

Working at the hospital, Bonnie had seen children die. She'd also seen what happened next.

She'd had a difficult time with Petra, almost forty hours of labour before the obstetrician finally allowed a cesarean. Five years, it was hard to fathom that that had been over five years ago. Later, with her morphine button, she'd drifted away from the pain into sleep, and an unconditional and unfamiliar joy. Because her staples began to tear, she'd been allowed to stay longer than most mothers in the hospital do. She woke one night to see Rick cradling Petra and he told her that nothing in the world was more important than the three of them in that room, and that he felt he understood the gaze of refugees, absent to everything except their narrow perch on the world holding a child.

After doing his rounds, and saying goodnight to his two girls in the hospital room, Rick would go home to Bonnie's parents who were visiting because of the new baby. Strangely, they'd been preparing their own meals that week, but would leave nothing for him. They were always asleep when he returned. It was as if they lived in a separate world from their son-in-law. Rick would make a sandwich, drink some beer and busy himself with e-mail, collapse on the futon downstairs with the dog. One night after Rick had left, Bonnie nursed Petra, who latched well, and a wave of confusing emotions swept over her. Joy mixed with grief. Cradling Petra's wonderfully smelling head, Bonnie couldn't help but imagining other women being forced to watch their children die.

Returning with the kids in the police car, Bonnie was blurred with shock. Yet, after he'd gotten home, Rick had insisted that they still go out for dinner. They'd almost had a fight when Bonnie had said that she didn't feel like going and Rick had stopped her from phoning the babysitter to cancel. She felt better when the kids had dragged Monica off to Petra's bedroom to play and Jack yelled for popcorn.

When they entered the restaurant's back door, she saw some friends sitting at a table, surely a coincidence, but then she knew the whole evening had been planned. She'd never had a surprise party. He'd done a fine job of keeping it from her; and with the exception of Anna, Rick's old university girlfriend, she'd have invited exactly the same people.

Talk of the war was banned, as was eventually the afternoon's events.

"Enough wine? Those are two words that just don't go together."

"This Grice guy's a naturalist, but he's not dry, I mean he's absolutely obsessed with insects, dangerous ones, and well, he's drawn to violent animals in general. Read the book, he's amazing. *The Red Hourglass*."

"The pickerel *is* good, you were right."

"You know, Gord, with an attitude like that it's too bad they don't let you wield a scalpel."

"The funniest thing I've ever seen, Dustin Hoffman is bowled over, I saw him on TV, he's laughing his guts out trying to tell this joke—so Donald Trump is interviewing this new secretary, and she says to him that she wants to suck his cock, and Trump looks at her and says, 'What's in it for me?'—I mean the joke's not that great, okay, it's all right, but the thing was, I mean, watching how it completely destroyed Dustin Hoffman, that was hilarious."

"It's like it never stops."

"How's Caitlin finding her new school?"

"You know, a resident told me that he loves working in Regina. He said that he'd never seen so many trauma wounds."

"Can you believe Kelleher?"

"Thank you so much, where did you find it? Look everybody, it's perfect."

"You may not believe it, but it's true, when you look at my husband, you're looking at someone who stole a car in New Jersey, got caught, and couldn't enter the States for five years. Naturally, this was before he met me. He never does things like that with me."

"A decaf please."

Bonnie had her second piece of cheesecake of the day, licked her fingers and used them to pick up some crumbs. When the cake had arrived, it had glowed with bright, burning magnesium, a birthday sparkler planted there by the restaurant staff.

A waiter rushed over and politely asked for help, someone was choking.

The restaurant was caught in that stalled frenzy when time transparently interrupts itself.

Anna and Rick got up. When they returned, Rick said something about the world being a goddamned hospital.

"No rest for we the wicked."

"Us, I think it should be us—no rest for us the wicked."

"Happy Birthday, Bonnie."

Driving home, Rick felt his good mood vanish when Bonnie advised him to slow down on the corner to their street. Last winter they'd spun a 360, and smashed into the yield sign, something the kids still talked about, though now they saw the accident as an astonishing accomplishment. Daddy killed the sign.

Bonnie quickly thanked him once again for the dinner party, but couldn't restrain herself.

"You shouldn't have forced me to go though, I mean, Petra could've . . ."

"But she's fine, they're both fine—why do you always, *always* see the worst?"

"That's not fair."

"I couldn't help it that I was called in."

"I'm not blaming you."

"Are you sure?"

"Look, it isn't fair to me that you continuously think that I hold you personally responsible for anything that happens. I tell you that the car's leaking antifreeze again and you act like I'm accusing you. I'm not; it's nobody's fault that the radiator needs repairing.

"Bonnie, we had a very agreeable evening, happy birthday, but leave it alone, okay."

She'd learned to ignore the myriad almost imperceptible cracks that threatened every marriage but only if you probed them. It's going to be too cold for the Santa Claus Parade tomorrow she said.

They parked at McDonalds, ate. It was rare that they did anything together the four of them as a family. They found a place on the northbound lanes of Albert Street. Cars had already lined the median's ditch, and lawn chairs were everywhere. After a half-hour, Bonnie had Rick take the kids back to wait in the car, it was so cold. She stayed by the road to keep her family a good spot to see floats.

If only the parade would start.

The difference between children and adults, Bonnie thought, is that they rely on the specific. Jack would add the parade to what he thought could happen in the world. And tomorrow he'll want to see the parade again. But adults can't live like that.

Some teenagers went by wearing blankets and pinkish-orange hair with the aura of neon. Only a few years ago they were kids just like hers. None of us can help it, Bonnie thought. Everything we experience tells us that nothing can be trusted, and yet we refuse to admit what we know. It is impossible to accept what we see.

Bonnie could just make out the lights of a police car moving toward her, so she turned to wave, but her family was already making its way to the roadside. Jack was so excited he didn't complain about having his nose wiped. The floats were nothing beside the pumper fire truck that passed by.

Three people drew up beside her, a father, presumably his daughter, and her near-pubescent daughter as well. They'd brought camping chairs that came out of canvas tubes. After they settled in, the man, with terribly broken teeth, dug out a large box of caramel popcorn, and offered it 'round. His hands were ravaged with eczema.

Some beauties in bikinis went by in a hot tub, something in the parade for the dads, the steam whisking over breasts and waving arms. Two years ago, Petra had run to hug the cartoon characters greeting the children with candy canes, but this year she was too sophisticated to join her brother by adding to the ring of children surrounding a green dinosaur.

When the man beside them spilled his popcorn on the dirt, and then shovelled it back into the box, giving some to Jack, Bonnie had enough. She lit into him. Some people were so incorrigibly stupid it was astonishing that they even bothered to live.

But that was hours ago.

It was story time, and Bonnie lay with one arm around Petra in her bedroom.

The first time Petra had laughed her baby laugh Bonnie had almost dissolved, and she'd heard that same laugh again tonight because a monster in a story had farted sparks before being revealed as merely the fantasies of a deeply paranoid rooster.

Petra's lava lamp looked like giant blood corpuscles, globs of liquid sun rising from the heat. There was a moment when the heat first released the liquid and it shot strands of gunk to the top that hovered there like specimens in formaldehyde or a nebula imprisoned in a glass tube. The light turned a plastic mother giraffe Bonnie had picked up at a yard sale into a shadow that seemed to look back at her.

Yesterday before everything happened, Sally the dog had eaten the legs and head off the baby giraffe, a toy that Petra hadn't played with for months, but she was inconsolable when she found it. They'd get another one, Bonnie promised, but that wouldn't do, it wouldn't be the same one, Petra said, it was the only one in the world, and the Mommy giraffe would know the difference.

But Then the Uncanny Put Its Hand on My Knee

— The jets come and go, but you can hardly hear them. Partially it's the music, but it must also have something to do with the thick glass they use in airport hotels. The air outside is stacked deep with moving planes. It must be A to Z up there for the people inside them—a business trip ends, a vacation begins, a girl with her Alice in Wonderland doll and comic books is visiting her divorced parent, someone died yesterday. What would you get if you could boil it all down to one sensation? What would be the underlying colour of all that experience if it were mixed together? The human blur. But thinking about other people doesn't get you very far. Nor do details, though I will concede that I love the heavy sturdiness of hotel-room curtains. These are some shade between green and unlit somnolent blue.

I've listened to the same song probably fifteen times now. How did people live before CD players? Tapes are so clumsy. Vodka's not my favourite, but that's what Lonny left last night. There was some beer in the fridge, but I wanted to bring a big bottle with me. Not that I usually drink that much, but the past thirty hours have been relentless.

Lonny, that bastard.

I've known him since catholic boys school, and should have said goodbye years ago, but I've always felt sorry for him. No more. He's a maniac. He often calls or drops over when he's pissed. Usually it's okay. I suppose that part of me likes to have someone to feel superior to. Before, I knew he was stupid, lost in self-pity, a loser who knew it, but after last night, I see that there's something evil there as well.

He killed my cat.

As a favour to me, he says. I'd gone to bed, left him to watch TV, drink, fall asleep on the couch, whatever, but I woke up to hear him washing his hands and mumbling shit, shit, shit. My bedroom's just off the kitchen. I'd been asleep an hour. He was falling down drunk, his hands were bleeding, and then he starts telling me that he's my only true friend, my best friend, and that I won't have to pay vet bills anymore. He knew they were crippling me, that my plastic's at its limits, and so he took care of things.

And then he wouldn't leave, he's crying, saying I couldn't kick him out, he was too drunk to drive—as if that had ever stopped him before. It was only when I told him that I was going to phone the cops and they'd charge him with torturing an animal that he took off. I did phone them then and let them know that I tried to stop this impaired guy from leaving my place, described his car and gave them Lonny's address.

You have to love animals to appreciate what Gus my cat meant to me. We've been buddies since my twenties. But his kidneys were shot, and I'd been giving him 150 ml of a hydrating solution intravenously every other day. He wasn't going to make it, but at least he'd been feeling better lately, he'd even caught a mouse last week.

I wasn't up to sticking my fingers in Gus's mouth to free the mouse, so I picked Gus up—he'd gotten so skinny it broke my heart—and carried him to the front door downstairs, and the mouse fell out of his mouth, but instead of going outside, the mouse followed the wall and ran underneath the door into my sister's apartment. She's got four cats, so it was out of the frying pan and into the fire.

The good thing is that she won't know it was me who let the mouse in.

Lonny's told me a number of times that I'm too soft, not enough of a man. All it's ever taken to shut him up is asking him about the last time he scored. Sometimes though, I suspect he's right in a way.

I didn't tell him the friendship was over when I should have. There were so many times that I'd reached my limit with him. Then I'd overlook everything. This sounds ridiculous, but he plays a good game of golf. We grew up together. And as I said, it doesn't hurt to have someone mediocre in your life.

My inertia didn't kill Gus, but it had some part in it.

My piss tonight smells like buttered popcorn, the hotel's wrinkled and scattered bedspread looks like a rough lake of poppies.

And I'd forgotten that, underneath it all, hotel rooms are faintly insulting. It's as if the sterilized glasses and paper strip across the toilet know that most of us are imposters—we act lazier than we would at home—but the entire hotel room knows that this rented luxury is completely unnatural. When you first walk in, the room announces that the only people who deserve to sully its space are well-heeled business travellers and lovers. Come on, I tell myself, quit being so stupid. I've got as much a right to be here as some executive with an expense allowance. Self-satisfied pricks, thinking that they deserve their success.

I've got to stop this sloppiness, thinking about failure this way pulls me apart. Just look at the planes. No, I can't do that either. I've come here to settle some things—but how do you control your own mind, make it its own target? I don't know what to do. Stalin once said that happiness was having an enemy, making him your friend, and then when he falls gently asleep on your breast, trusting you, grateful for you, you stab him.

But this hotel room is no Russian dacha.

I've only had power over my mind once. When we were teenagers, a friend of mine and I spent the weekend waiting in line to buy Rolling Stones tickets. We set up camp on Friday, the tickets went on sale Monday morning. Every couple of hours we'd shovel back some bennies so we wouldn't fall asleep. With the beans we could smoke up as much as we wanted, drink, watch every single minute of the zoo because that's what the lineup became—a zoo. There were a few hundred of us eventually and pretty well everyone was wasted. At least we were given numbers, like we were waiting at a deli counter in a supermarket, so there was some order. The thing is—whether it was the drugs or lack of sleep I don't know—reality became porous. Nothing stayed intact. In the middle of Sunday night, it was like walking into a dream the city was having about itself. Finally Monday came and the ticket office opened and I'd been walking around the street when I heard my friend call out to me. I looked up, there were cops around for crowd control, and at the top of the stairs was Andy yelling for me to come up. It was now our turn; if I didn't buy the tickets then, I'd never be able to get them. Except that I couldn't tell whether I was hallucinating or not. I'd learned earlier that night not to trust what I saw, so I stood and stared up the stairs, trying to determine if what I was seeing was actually there. The bravest thing I've ever done was to put my foot forward on that concrete staircase.

For all I knew, the stairs would change, ripple into a car heading my way. To gamble on reality is to step between neurons that can't distinguish shadows from rain. I forced myself to go up the stairs.

So I learned I had metaphysical guts.

I also found out that other people loved the Stones, which doesn't sound like much, but the world has many ways of showing you your limitations. How things aren't the way you'd like them to be. I'd always thought that Mick was speaking precisely to me, revealing things in his songs that only I really understood. Then this aristocrat showed up—chin-length black hair, looking androgynous like Jagger himself, a dishevelled coat, fine, fine hands that eventually smashed a display case to get a Stones poster; for the rest of the time there he wore this emerald-coloured cloth around his fists to stop the bleeding. He was much better than the rest of us. He brought a woman with him who turned out to be his sister. She was slight and dark, whisked out of a Berlin dive in the '30s, someone you could feel your cock aching for—and true to imagination, she eventually crawled under a blanket she'd brought and blew one of the guys in the lineup. Everybody pretended they weren't staring at this pretty ordinary looking fellow, and he kept his eyes closed while moving her head up and down beneath the blanket. It was while she was giving this guy head that her brother smashed the glass to get the poster. The thing is, I knew that Jagger would have found this brother–sister team much more to his taste than me. I'd have done anything to be either of them, my love was so conventional and tame. And now what? He probably sells life insurance and she's married with kids, working in a travel agency part-time.

And yet, at the time, the brother and sister duo were dazzling. Almost feral. Only excess held sway over them. Does their misplaced beauty still matter? I hate asking questions like that; part of my problem is this incorrigible sentimentality—but how do I get rid of it?

And I can't accept that time happens the way it does like everyone else seems to do. Everyone I've met just lets things go, and then they get on with it.

I think I know what Lonny was feeling when he killed Gus.

When I was a kid, my sister and I sat with Dad in bed one Easter and watched *The Robe*. We'd gotten to stay up late and eat chocolate bars as a treat. Coffee Crisps. I remember Caligula having a slave tortured on the rack. The next morning I took one of my GI Joes and put him in my dad's vice-grips down in his workshop. As I crushed the plastic doll, broke through to the springs attaching his limbs, I was astonished to feel a completely new emotion. It was a dull, almost metallic, invitation to destroy something I loved. A thick, thick, joyful grief. If Lonny found it temporarily entertaining to destroy our friendship, he was probably too drunk to recognize that it will damage him more than me.

Children are familiar with pretty well the entire emotional spectrum, so coming across something different took me by surprise. Since then, I've only added two more kinds of feeling to the repertoire—sexual jealousy and whatever it is that constitutes aesthetic experience. A few days after I smashed my toy, my mother came rushing in from cleaning up the garden, yelling for me. She'd found three of my GI Joes; they'd been crucified, red Magic Marker staining their hands and feet. Why my parents didn't send me to a psychiatrist, I'll never know.

It's not important. I haven't turned into a sociopath. Not that talking with a shrink would've done much. Not one human being in a hundred can actually change. Coaching myself to get it right, to recreate how it must have sounded the first time Maggie read it to herself, fresh from the Muse, I go over this poem again.

Requiem
The press didn't cover it
How yesterday a woman & her
Two lovers were found
In the bottom of a child's pool
Changed into three orange fish

Now iced & gaping & marble-eyed
On display for public perusal
All but one winking occasionally
At the casual onlooker beneath
The sign advertising wicker cages

Which is where one of them
Sits and stares, fine as stonework
Having only today promised
To give me lessons in
The art of elocution.

It's not a real poem, I mean, it's never been published as far as I know. Maggie wrote it for a writing class a little more than fourteen years ago. I like the poem, which surprised me then, and still does, given that I was one of the two men metamorphosized into a goldfish. I don't know if she'd begun sleeping around when she composed the poem, but I guiltily went through her portfolio for clues the night she spent away from our apartment, doing mushrooms and then banging the guy she was supposedly studying with for her art history final.

We'd been living together for almost three years, were planning on getting married. Back then Maggie was going to be a poet, her job being, she once told me, to correct distortions. I didn't know what I wanted, but I was going to shape my life so that it would blaze like the flash of a camera at night, a hundred cameras bursting out, burning up and down the void.

Don't misunderstand me; I'm not completely fixated on the past.

I've not sitting here, in this hotel room decorated with inane sepia pastorals on the wall, drinking lukewarm vodka, because I'm lamenting something that happened in my twenties. At least not exactly. The thing is, tonight, before I came here, completely out of the blue, Maggie phoned me, though she calls herself Margaret now. It wasn't just her telling me about her new baby. When I heard about her two divorces, move to Spain, new marriage, more about the baby, learned that she's earning over a hundred and fifty grand a year because of her expertise as a lawyer for Christ's sake, something went out inside.

I had to go somewhere. I needed to do something perfectly gratuitous. I had to retreat into the next several hours, maybe even the next day, so I grabbed my CD player, the right music, and got a cab to the airport.

The cabbie could tell I didn't want to make small talk. What a dismal way to earn a living. Cab drivers must be reborn spirits working off some shit they did in a past life. Because it was late, we got to the airport strip quickly. The fare wasn't too bad, but I put it on Visa anyway. The irony isn't lost on me that I'm likely the only person who's ever stayed in this hotel room who's neither getting off nor on a plane.

I don't know how it is for other men, but everything I've learned that's important, women have taught me.

Why should I consent to my life?

Here are some facts. The only jobs I've had have been moronic. Meter reader. Clerk in a porn store. And now I work for an alternate phone company, trying to get people to leave Ma Bell. According to shareholders, this is serious, important work. I don't have a wife, kids, or house. It took me a decade to get a BA. Nothing has ever really grabbed me. After taking courses in anthropology, film, psychology, literature, I eventually had enough credits to graduate with a minimal degree in philosophy. When my dad, an obstinate, almost psychotically unimaginative man, died, he left me enough to live on for one year. Dad wanted me to do some volunteer work—it sounds good in a job interview he'd said—and study for law school. This was to be my second chance, he wrote in his final letter to me, but what right did he have to be my judge? Dad was a man who'd never once suspected how strange things can become, and that nothing on a resumé is what finally matters.

It's impossible to say who you are, but I can say that I know something about music, and it seems I've finally learned how to talk to women—imagine T.S. Eliot impersonating Jack Nicholson. With only a typewriter, I used to write letters for Amnesty International. I'm honest enough to say that cellulite leaves me cold. It's also true that I occasionally send money to kids in the war zones. I also take the time to notice things. This morning, before I knew I was going to spend the night next to an airport, I willed myself to remember those two teenage girls trying to spell their boyfriends' names from the subway transfers. Who else will remember their doing that? They won't. Here's another fact. Customers buying porn are very formal.

—Is this the dildo you're interested in sir, the burgundy one?

—Yes, that's right, I think I'll take that one, thank you.

And then this usually middle-aged man goes out into the street with two penises, though one has straps. Imagine the war stories those penises will eventually tell each other. But it's easy to say true things—what does it mean not to lie?

It's accurate that not long after Maggie/Margaret called I put some CDs in a suitcase and came here, but it's not the entire story. My sister had a fight with her daughter earlier tonight. I could hear words with an ugly ring of permanence to them, words like slut, abortion, and bitch being tossed back and forth. I sat on the stairs to listen better, feeling bad for my niece. I've had standoffs in the past with my sister and I know how difficult she can get. Then my sister cries out, "You just don't get it, do you? You're going to end up a failure just like everybody else in this family." This wasn't aimed directly at me, but it may as well have been a hand grenade.

I can't change the fact that our society turns on people like me, judges us, and then spits us out on the sidewalk. But Christ, to be a failure in this culture should be a badge of honour. Ask the greats—Beckett, Dylan. But they don't know ordinary failure those guys; they've never felt the run-of-the-mill terror of never getting a good job. They don't wake up every single morning feeling the Atlantic Ocean on top of your brain—and the ocean is this— maybe, maybe, maybe I'll have to make up my mind and agree with everyone else that what sits here is simply mediocrity. After hearing my sister rant, I lay down on the bathroom floor. Right beside me is Gus's old litter box. It was too much. I heard a plane go overhead and I had to be there.

Go to the airport, get a hotel room, find out what's going on. This is one more move for Hegel's World Spirit; I mean, who's ever done anything like this before?

But when the taxi pulled up to the hotel tonight, there was this woman waiting for a cab. I've never seen anything like it. She must have been in a car crash. Her left hand was a tiny ball of charred flesh, literally the size of a golf ball, her other hand was a plastic stick, her left wrist the size of a garden hose. We met eyes by accident. She was with another woman, probably her sister, who held the luggage. The damaged woman wore pants, a cheap floral top, even a hat, the other a dress; that's all I took in.

Why did I have to see this? There's nothing I can do to help her and I already know that there's hurt in the world. Seeing something like that makes me hate life a little more, then I return to my own concerns. My mother calls people like that "God's reminders." Yeah, fine, Mom. Summed up, my mother's life demonstrates that you can live for decades being a harmless enemy to all that's sentient.

My dad believed that everyone gets what they deserve, but that's because he was so full of himself. Just after I saw the mutilated woman, I overheard some girls in school uniforms talking at the hotel registry, two of them were very hot, and one of them was saying, "And we met this really nice guy, his name was, I can't remember his name, but he was like—" but then she saw me looking at her, probably thought I was imagining her naked, except that I must have looked as if I've got one foot in the grave today, so they moved away.

It's true, I bet that she's growing some nice fat nipples, but does she deserve them? And they'll be a beautiful, neon butterfly pink— that must be the vodka talking. There's no telling how the world will look at you.

I swim at the local pool. When I was a kid, indoor pools were austere. Doing lengths, you felt comfortably alone in a vast, shimmery trap for echoes, but the one I swim at now has got fountains, immense foam dinosaur skeletons hanging from the ceiling, plastic plants, piped-in music. I once asked a woman at the pool if she knew the names of any of the dinosaurs overhead. She looked up, said that she hadn't really noticed them before, and then added, "that's easy, there's a triceratops."

"And you?" she asked me. "What kind of dinosaur are you?"

"A Rex," I said. We started chatting, and I've gone out a few times with her. Her name's Toni. Maybe I'll call her tonight.

But I keep seeing women who've suffered terribly.

Not so long ago I spotted a woman at the pool who must have been one of those thalidomide kids. She was swimming on her back in the slow lane, very muscular, flippers for hands and feet, wearing goggles and water-cap. The water would submerge her face, but she forced herself through the pool, furiously, furiously determined. She's from my generation. It was a gnarled, rigorous ballet. Meanwhile this old man emerged out of the hot tub with a gargantuan, absolutely white toenail. It was whiter than Styrofoam. Young beauties strutted by, pulling at their bathing suit bottoms, the way they always do, the water greasy on my skin, the air steamy with chlorine. I've changed the times when I go swimming, so I don't see that poor woman with the flippers anymore, but I watched her do half a dozen lengths that night.

In plain English, I don't have anything to show for my life, but it's more than that. Okay, I pay attention to things, but my life has no trajectory. Maggie's does. Her prior life has paid off; she climbed out of her weird childhood, struggled through student life and debt, her marriages. Now her life makes sense, the past has been *for* something; the future's not a complete blank. The woman waiting for the cab tonight must simply divide her existence into before and after her accident; the swimmer had her life story determined right from the start. But for me, time has only been time; I was looking around for a while and then at some point my life dissolved.

I didn't even have a chance.

Maggie pictures a lovers' triangle in her poem, which isn't really the way it was. It wasn't only her who had second thoughts about our getting married. There were moments when I looked at her and it seemed as though we didn't owe each other anything. That morning, when I knocked on the residence door, took in her eyes as she sat up in the narrow bed by the window, her white shirt and blue pants on the floor, for a long blurred second I couldn't believe my luck. I could have this day as a gift, a way of starting a different life, but oh God, I couldn't help choosing instead to give into a sorrow that's followed me into these years that weren't supposed to happen.

Maggie covered herself with a sheet, and ordered me to close the door, wait in the hall. When we got back at our apartment, she was guilt to my virtue—she cried for over an hour—and then I fucked her. We were so unforgivably young that when she agreed to have sex, she warned me not to go down on her. Yeah, okay. Jesus. I guess we were all a little tired that night. I couldn't believe she'd say that. How could she possibly have thought that I was going to kiss her pussy after her lover had cum inside her? After, I threw every one of her perfume bottles into the bedroom mirror. We'd given each other a few hundred days, and they all drained away that morning, an inaudible party.

It's true that breaking mirrors isn't wise; since then everything's been either a latent mistake, or a return to an old one, or just unbelievable.

I see Maggie in this other guy's bed, she tells me to leave, so I go into the men's room, throw water on my face, urinate. In comes her lover, he looks at me, then goes over and he takes his morning piss. Later, I asked Maggie why she wanted me out of the room and she tells me that she didn't want the picture of her getting naked out of another man's bed to be in my head forever. Can you believe the symmetry? He screws her, I piss, he pisses, and then it's my turn with her. And meanwhile, my so-called wife-to-be tries to protect me from discouraging images.

Only a few days before Maggie broke our lives apart, it was April thirteenth, I think a Tuesday, that previous weekend we'd been home for Easter. While helping her load the dishwasher—I can still feel this, it's like the exact inward stab you feel in your lungs when you've come down with pneumonia—she says that maybe we should put off getting married just a little while. Mom later tells me that all brides get cold feet, not to worry.

Later that autumn, after she'd discovered that, among other things, her lover didn't understand Patti Smith, we went out for dinner a few times, and Maggie started letting me know that we were getting close to moving back in together. She was living in our old apartment and I had a bachelor's suite downtown. When the lease expired for our old apartment, the two of us could find a new place together. But one night she had one of our mutual friends over for dinner. He'd been introduced to us actually by Andy, my Rolling Stones buddy, and though I liked this other guy—he had the nerve to sit in a tree one night and shoot out the windows of his high school—I once saw him pick Maggie up, lift her by the hips, and there was something in the gesture that made me realize I'd have to keep my eyes wide, wide open. I knew when she told me she was inviting him to her apartment that they'd somehow sleep together, and as the story goes, he went into her bedroom around five in the morning, her bedroom which once was ours, and that was that. I'd spent the night trying to force myself to sleep, listened to the radio because I couldn't stand my music collection anymore. Nothing I did could make me believe that the night would eventually end.

Back then, the FM stations were always playing this one jeremiad addressed to an unfaithful woman, but it was also a ragged hymn that said, 'piss off,' to the entire cosmos. I held onto that song, phoned in to a couple of rock stations several times to get them to replay it. I've heard this song innumerable times since, but only a year ago, this friend of Andy's phones me from a plane—Jesus, must everyone I know have it made in the shade—Andy's friend phones and his connection's been delayed and can I meet him at the airport? Why not, I thought. I can do that. He and I had smoothed things over, over a decade had happened, but then the uncanny put its hand on my knee. As I drove out to the airport, naturally the same song came on the radio.

I don't believe in cosmic irony, or that anything genuinely repeats itself, but what is the probability of such a coincidence? How can life be so banal? And yet, think about it: how many steps weren't taken by how many people to ensure this symmetry occurred? Classic, the way time and its rhythms dump on you, golden showers from the gods. What kind of costume are you supposed to put on in the morning when your life shows you mirrors when there are none?

I turned up the radio as loud as I could and let go with the lyrics, knowing most of them by heart.

This isn't the first time I've reread Maggie's poems.

When we broke up I asked her for copies, don't ask me why.

Only about six months after she'd married for the first time,

Maggie met me in this Polish restaurant we used to frequent, the Staropolska. Her life was a mess, she tells me, she can't bear her older husband—he's an alcoholic, she'd found him in the bathtub with a student, a young man—and if I'll take her back, she'll come. It was October twenty-fifth; we ate perogies, schnitzel, and drank vodka, neat, as she liked it. Maggie tells me that I should stop wearing a jacket, white shirt, and black pants—I don't need to go through life looking like I'm a newspaper reporter she says—Maggie tells me that she'll make her break that weekend.

I got on the subway like Mary Poppins flying in for a visit, feeling that I'd been wrong, utterly wrong about just about everything. I could feel joy again. It was getting close to rush hour and I must have been emanating light.

That evening I broke up with my girlfriend, a woman whose skin, incidentally, gave off the smell of evergreens after rain. I've never found skin like that again. As soon as I sat down at the table in our favourite pub, even before I ordered anything, even before I spoke to her, my girlfriend knew. "What did she say to you?" she asked, announced, accused.

That night I went over Maggie's portfolio, especially that damned poem about the fish in wicker cages. It was like the words changed in front of my eyes as they drew the world apart and made it come together again, but this time the right way.

Maggie didn't come to my door that weekend. She never has. Even in dreams it's the same thing—she's going to return, then it all disappears, and once again she's refused without a word to come home.

Maggie, I adored you.

I need to go very slowly.

Part of me knows that the past extends nowhere. As soon as a moment dies, you're alone, pressed up against a space that has never even slightly existed. The future's a vapour trail that points only to what hasn't happened. I also know that it can't be like this; maybe our entire lives are indelibly present in each moment, but we're never able to see it. That's why I have to go back to the poem. It has to hold something of me, the real me that made us eggs for breakfasts in those egg cups we bought in Toledo, the real me ghosting the corner of the page as she finished the poem. The me that I took away from myself.

Vodka makes me hear in bits and pieces. Hours of planes have gone by. No matter how hard I try, I can't get close to this thing.

It's now five AM and Fauré's *Requiem* has been playing. Music has always ruled me, but music is a syringe. How can one voice pack a million, billion lives into the four minutes of "Pie Jesu"? Their ache may as well be the marshmallow salad my mother insists on making for family gatherings. Lonny's vodka has turned into sodium pentothal inside me, liquid spidery gauze that turns you toward the truth. How can he drink the stuff? He must not do it right. Do I phone in sick, or just quit my day job? But before I go to sleep, could there be anything better for seeing my lady Toni tonight than ordering a porn film through the hotel's cable? Toni, Toni. Unruly thing that she believes herself to be, with her toys and little requests—amazing they let her teach kindergarten. But they do, they do. Born and raised a WASP in Toronto, she can't even speak proper English.

—I hate being depraved of you, she once actually said.

—I love being depraved with you, I told her, making Toni sharpen her face at me, 'til I told her I was only teasing. Toni darling, I said, I'm only teasing you, ssshh.

Just So

— Liz is watching her daughter Sandy playing in the sandbox her husband had built. The two-year-old is convalescing from a trip to the hospital. She'd become so dehydrated from the flu that she had to be put on an IV unit for almost two days. Liz believed that she would never forget the nurse's freckled arm, the look on her husband's face as they held their screaming baby down while the nurse made four separate attempts to find a vein, eventually securing one on a tiny foot.

Liz is calmer than her husband about these things; when she saw how hard Sandy had fought, she knew that she'd be okay, truly sick children are listless. Dan had insisted that he be allowed to stay in Sandy's hospital room overnight, but today he's back on the road, doing a run down into the States. Liz is expecting, and her young husband hates to leave her alone so much, but she feels fine she keeps telling him, hiding how much she despises living in the townhouse complex.

Everyone is too poor and grasshoppers are everywhere this summer.

Most of the children are simply put outside all day; every so often a door opens and a mother shouts out her child's name into the adjoining yards the children have made their own. Liz has made friends with Jeannie who lives beside her, but Jeannie's little boy, now four years old and talking to a grasshopper cupped in his hands, says all that you need to know about life next door.

"Get away from me you bastard," he mutters to the grasshopper, "I'm going to squish your nipples out."

And then there was Jeff, the most beautiful child she'd ever seen, and spoiled, too, by his grandparents, who bend over backward for their daughter-in-law because of the shame they spend on their son, who'd drunkenly crashed his snowmobile through ice up north two years ago. Jeff says that the only thing he remembers about his father is that he was always puking a lot; but today, Jeff's sporting a stunning Superman outfit, the soft material glistening in the sun, the clean, red cape turning slowly in the breeze. He could be a commercial for laundry detergent. All the women tell his mother that Jeff's going to turn some heads someday.

In the centre of a knot of children, Jeff wildly impresses them by eating a grasshopper. Howls of joy rise up from the kids. When Liz eventually cottons on to what's happening, he's on his third, and as she drags him over to his townhouse and rings the doorbell, she doesn't see Sandy climbing out of the sandbox with a box of what she calls her "apple goose."

So much of a child's life is invisible.

Sandy zigzags over to the hollyhocks. There is no difference between what's alive and what isn't. A cascade of three massive, pink flowers have weighed down a stalk, pushed it almost to the ground, so that the little girl can reach up and touch them.

"Mommy, Daddy, Sandy," she names the flowers, and then she makes her way back to the sandbox and pushes Raymond, her rhino, through the sand. Her world's spinning and translucent, a constant cluster of new words and things. Everything is sentient. Sandy sees that a hugely blue, not yellow, sky is falling out of the tree in their yard, and she's just recently understood what it means *to like* something, and she knows that Raymond likes sand, Raymond likes sand.

But days are tissue thin, only two or three can cling together at a time. Some dreams have more substance and persistence. Twenty years later, those children have grown up and everyone that lived in the townhouses has moved many times. Including Liz and Sandy. Liz rarely thinks about her past. So little remains. These days, if she tried, she'd have trouble coming up with more than one or two her neighbours' names from when Sandy was a baby.

Her noon-to-eight shift at Jimmy's Restaurant and Tavern was almost over, and Liz was hungry. She emptied a single serving box of Rice Krispies into a cup, added some milky coffee and stirred everything up, a treat that repelled the others.

"Is there a lid for this jar?" asked the new girl, Janice, leaning up against the bar, rubbing her toes against the back of her calf, nylon against nylon.

A few customers lined the bar gazing up into the TV, but at least it wasn't like the one downstairs in the poolroom that played porn all day, a new gimmick that was possibly working, but then, it was too soon to tell.

"Good night tonight?" asked Jimmy, years of peppermint schnapps and boredom mingling on his breath. "At least somebody's making money." Liz had never met a businessman who didn't perpetually cry the blues.

Like many women of her generation, Liz was divorced, had eventually switched to a lighter brand of cigarettes, and found herself with a daughter still living at home.

She paid her float back to the bartender, arranged her tips, and began her complimentary staff drink, a rum and coke. She mentioned to Janice, a girl far too young to be working in this kind of bar, that her daughter Sandy was out for the evening. Liz too was glad that this wasn't Texas, where according to today's newspaper, guns kill more people than cars do.

Safely home in her apartment, Liz changed her clothes, scrubbed the old beer from beneath her fingernails. When she was alone, she loved talking to her life-sized ceramic bust of Johnny Cash, the way others enjoy houseplants. She went over her day, taking time to read him their horoscopes. He's Pisces, she's Gemini. Guess we better stay away from Texas, she suggested, though she's never had the slightest desire to go there, but Nashville, that's a different story.

She ate her lasagna cold from the margarine container, and read the apartment newsletter that had been in the mailbox. Tenants were reminded once again not to hang flags or put tinfoil in their windows. She didn't bother heating up her supper because they were saying now that only genuine microwave dishes were safe; besides, leftovers tasted best straight from the fridge.

The lasagna came from a group she'd recently joined, Women Without Men. The six women got together once a month; when it was your turn to be hostess, you had to make enough food so that everyone could take home one meal that wouldn't have to be prepared the following week. There was only one rule—you had to accept that what's over is over.

They'd decided this after Carol had spoken one night about her husband. Dying of cancer, his bones were so weak that he'd broken his arm by simply bumping the rail by the side of his bed, and yet, just as the cancer was about to kill him, he'd offered Carol a younger man's wink—an extraordinary and terrible gift that Liz secretly envied. At their next meeting they'd all agreed that the past was off limits. But it wasn't that simple, the present was risky too—Sheila hated talk about children, and Evie curled up inside if someone put something extra in their coffee, or got anyone tipsy on wine at lunch.

Liz told Johnny Cash about the new girl, tore into one of the customers, and did some slap-dash dusting with her serviette, cleaning beneath some souvenirs she'd kept from Sandy's childhood—a wooden block with an orange S, a plastic, very life-like grey rhinoceros named Raymond, a doll's tiny ironing board. She wondered aloud about her daughter. Raising a daughter meant living your girlhood over again, except this time through there was more to worry about. But Johnny helped; there was nothing that man didn't know. Least of which was, life is a very, very open and unruly book.

Liz had gotten into the habit of tidying up on a daily basis ever since Amanda from upstairs had begun visiting. Some people could unravel the secrets of cards or tea leaves, others your palm, but Amanda was unconventional. She could read beds. With a number of success stories to her credit, she could tell a person's future from the shape their body left in the sheets. Incredible, but true—blankets, a piece of hair, indentations in a pillow, but mostly the body's outline held moments from the future for someone who knew about such things.

Amanda had suggested coming over on a Sunday because she had to look at a bed as soon as you woke up, but on Sundays Sandy liked to sleep in, so Liz had arranged for Amanda to drop by early one workday morning. They had coffee and cigarettes in the living room that was also a bedroom, her neighbour quiet and unsmiling at first, a clairvoyant in blue silk pajamas with a taste for fancy perfume. After turning the radio off and washing her hands, Amanda immersed herself in her work. She'd been immediately taken by surprise.

"I begin by looking back," she said, "but I don't understand. There's nothing here, not a single thing."

"Is that bad?"

"I don't know. I've never come across this before."

Not a single thing. Normally she could sense images from a person's previous time on the planet, but that morning nothing—which was impossible, because the Akashic records hold absolutely everything that's ever happened. But there it was. In Liz's previous incarnation she'd been someone of whom nothing at all remained.

Next time, though, it was going to be completely different, Amanda had claimed, on her hands and knees beside the pullout bed, running her hand over the sheets, gathering precise strands from the future. Next time, according to certain cosmic laws, she'd come back as a man. Amanda could see her friend clearly; someone famous being interviewed through a huge two-way TV screen in a gorgeous apartment filled with paintings, bizarre-looking statues, and what looked like an immense terrarium beneath a window. That will be the way they do things then. Liz didn't believe a word of it, but good news was good news, wherever it came from. The idea of a terrarium appealed to her.

"Now, before you ask me whether I do this sort of thing for myself," Amanda had offered, "let me tell you right now that it doesn't work that way, okay."

Amanda and Liz had taken to renting disaster videos.

Before, Amanda had frequented malls, then the market, and the library downtown, favourite spots of hers, but these places quickly receded into that watered-down, loosened look that had begun to cover pretty well everything these days. When she'd discovered that she loved to rent movies, especially those popular ones that were watched over and over again, she felt wonderful again because she could feel all the pairs of eyes that had also watched what she was seeing on the screen. She loved being in a video store, among the life-sized posters, the people browsing, feeding from brown paper bags of popcorn.

Unable to afford as many videos as she would like, she and Liz often took turns renting from the small place down the street, which had the added bonus of making them feel virtuous, since the store wasn't part of a chain, but belonged to someone who lived in the neighbourhood. Every so often she'd take the owner's advice, but usually his recommendations turned out to be more cryptic than fun.

Terry, the video store owner, was, as Liz liked to say, a character. A one-time biker, then a laid-off sheet metal worker who'd managed to buy a dying video business, he looked like the sort of man whose photograph was stored in a police computer system. Where the skin on his arms wasn't covered with tattoos there were scars. As he handed out flavoured popcorn to his customers he'd also offer impromptu movie reviews. When a customer came into the store, he'd glance at their viewing history on the computer screen.

Watching three, sometimes four movies a day, Terry had become an expert. To his amazement, he found himself building up his foreign selection. He bought them mostly for himself; these movies rarely left the store. It was good that no one from the old days could see him now. Whenever anyone rented a horror film, he'd ask why it was that people hated to see animals killed but didn't mind watching teenagers being carved up by psychotics in hockey masks. He'd told Amanda that before he'd bought the business he'd suspected that most people were stupid, but running a video store had removed any doubts.

When Liz brought *Titanic* to his makeshift office at the back of the store, he said: "Big ship. Lots of people die. Too many dumb jokes. Cameron tries to be clever with a Model T. The iceberg gets away."

Liz and Amanda thought the movie was sublime.

After they'd sat through most of the closing credits, they talked about the older woman seeing the drawing of her younger, dazzling self, hidden for a lifetime beneath the ocean.

The part that stayed with them though was that gruesome bit near the end which showed corpses floating upright in life-jackets, lightly covered with the night's frost, a mother still holding her child, both frozen and bobbing quietly in the waves. When Liz said that she'd never seen anything like that, that she felt indecent looking at those poor people, Amanda agreed, but when she'd seen the bodies in the water, her gift had unexpectedly awoken.

The image of trenches at night flashed across her mind. There was an unmistakable connection. Something, Amanda knew, had snapped in the invisible air surrounding the unsinkable ship and a few years later, the Germans had started using mustard and chlorine gas.

All evening, Liz had been waiting for the right moment to let Amanda in on some treasured family lore. When her grandfather had emigrated from England, someone had tried to sell him a steerage ticket on the *Titanic*, but he'd taken another ship. This made watching the movie pretty strange.

"Perverse," said Amanda. She was about to say that families were not really families anyway, not even parents were connected to their children in reality, but knowing how Liz felt about her daughter, she simply said that it must have been creepy to watch the boat go down.

"That's not the half of it," replied Liz.

"You need some *Titanic* stuff to add to your collection," Amanda said, taking in her friend's belongings—postcards spreading from the fridge into the living room, vases stuffed with oddities on a bookshelf, a petite glass hand whose fingers held rings, even an Arab astride a camel beside a miniature, though living, oasis, the perfect Mother's Day present from last spring.

"I'm not interested in morbid things like that," Liz replied, "my collection is meant to remind me of good things. Tell me something about your day."

"I was at the library this morning," Amanda said, "and I stood behind this woman taking out three books—lessons in calligraphy, a self-help book on grief, another on beauty tips for women aged fifty. Some poor man's going to get a fancy letter from a woman wearing too much makeup."

"Amanda, I'm worried about Sandy. She can't find a really good job. She doesn't have anyone special in her life. Without someone paying attention, you begin to slip away. Especially when you're young."

"What about when you're old?"

"I'm not so old. I'm not even close to fifty. Sometimes I do feel as though I'm missing out. But I can look after myself."

"Sandy will be fine, Liz."

"How do you know? You haven't read her bed," she teased.

"I can just tell. Trust me. But I've got to get some sleep."

"Sweet dreams, Amanda."

"Nightie-night."

As she stood up to say goodbye, Amanda could see hundreds of images pressing from the inside against the TV screen now that the set had been turned off. Most of them were people trying to claw their way out.

That night Liz dreamed that her ex-husband had taken her downstairs into the basement—though she noted to herself within the dream that they'd never had a proper basement—to show her a little room that he'd turned into a plane's cockpit. He invited her into the small room aglow with instrument panels. There were hundreds of variously coloured lights flashing. It was cramped, but comfortable, because what was important was out there in front of them.

She sat down as they backed up out of the sharply inclined driveway, past the pine trees in their yard, and taxied to the end of the absolutely silent street. It was sleeting. She'd seen their name and house number painted on a white plaque suspended from a post, then an animal hanging beneath the sign, a tiny, exact elephant she determined. Almost at the dead end, where the water was, she could see their street had turned into a bay, with lights on the other side of the shore barely visible.

Liz kept thinking "this is a toy, this is just a toy," but she envied him this magic retreat, this game that was always there waiting, ready for him in their basement when he wanted to disappear.

Out over the water now, she could see imitation frozen fish deep beneath the ocean waves. It was like flying into a diorama at a museum. He turned the nose of the plane out over the embankment. Worried about what kind of dream this was going to turn out to be, she checked to make sure the propellers were running. They were, and she was immediately thrilled, utterly elated as all at once they were flying, first for a while just above the turbulent, obviously filmed whitecaps, briefly chasing a red speedboat ahead of them as it rose and fell with the waves, and then up into the sky with droplets of water on the plane's windscreen.

It was so astonishingly real and patently a toy at the same time, it was glorious. Just as she awoke, Liz knew what her husband was doing; he was welcoming her into the ordinary secrets of men.

Liz's daughter Sandy was a caller for a telemarketing agency that raised funds for a charity. Most nights she felt lucky just to face a window at work; but tonight she was jubilant. Nearly everyone else sat in front of walls covered with signs whose slogans were written in blue magic marker. She came in twice a day, for the morning and evening shifts. Nine to one, five to nine. In between she slept, watched a little television, occasionally went out for lunch. Students, for the most part, surrounded her, and teacher's aids, though a mysteriously disgraced lawyer came in for a while during the mornings. A young, unemployable geologist had recently left to join the army.

Turnover was swift—it was very hard to make a living on the phones—and the long-timers kept to themselves, except for a cheerful, pony-tailed writer who'd written a manifesto in which, he claimed, several publishers had shown an interest. But they wanted a different title. *Between Black and White* wasn't good enough apparently. His idea was that nothing was absolute, everything was a pale shade of grey. Whenever anyone new started on the job, he cornered them during a break. On her first miserable night he'd shown Sandy the rolled up manuscript that he kept in a backpack and asked her whether she'd read it and make some recommendations.

The morning supervisor was caught in dreams of commercial grandeur, having once worked for Visa, managing collection accounts. Repeatedly cautioning her callers to put a smile in their voices, she came to work in a business suit and perfect manicure. Although no one they called could see anyone in the office, she still pushed the manager for a dress code. She constantly calculated their progress, and felt miserable if they couldn't match the amount raised by the night shift the evening before. It was an unfair contest, though. Although they were crankier, more people answered the phone at night. If one of her callers reached the official quota, she'd write a higher number down on top of the page where they logged calls. Bags of potato chips were given as rewards. Getting someone to make a pledge with a credit card meant a dollar bonus. Failing to follow the script meant a reprimand.

The night supervisor was a washed-out grad student in sweats who enjoyed haranguing the teenage girls. Usually holed up in her office, she read underground comic books, fantasizing revenge against a capitalist culture that didn't have any interest in her brains.

If Sandy made twenty-five calls an hour, it seemed that twenty-three said no. People on the other end couldn't imagine the continuous rejection. Every time she dialed she felt fear, anticipation, contempt, and utter loneliness. And it was weird, too, talking to so many people in a day. Then there were those very few people who actually were happy to hear her voice. Until she'd gotten the job, she'd had no idea how many folks were rotting in their homes, waiting for someone, anyone, to call. To these miserable people, even a telemarketer was welcome. And then you had to fight to get them off the line.

She sat beside Doug, who'd offer her assurances in between calls, his coffee-glazed voice seductive to people who would've hung up on her. He'd been working there for almost a year, but unless you knew him well it didn't show. The morning supervisor called him "The Tin Man," because she understood his sarcasm as terrible heartlessness. Doug wore a T-shirt emblazoned with a marine blasting away with a machine gun, beneath it the logo: "Kill 'em all. Let God sort them out." After a few weeks Sandy and Doug began to flirt, but not seriously, only as a game, his marriage an acknowledged safety zone between them. As each weekend approached, they'd joke that this was the one they'd go out for their big date.

Tonight Sandy was on top of the world. Not only had she made her quota, this would be her last shift. She'd managed to get a new job.

One of those monster bookstores had just opened and she'd been hired. At first it would be simply selling coffee and picking up after customers, but during the interview she'd been told that there was room for advancement if she did well. At least it was something closer to what her mother considered respectable work, though Liz would surprise her daughter by believing that these stores placed surveillance cameras in the washrooms, not to catch shoplifters, but people masturbating with the store's collection of erotica.

It was delicious spurning the night supervisor's request for two weeks notice. Sandy would make a slightly big deal out of her announcement when she, Doug, and a couple of others went for drinks, something they always did on Friday nights. She let Doug in on the good news in his car. Genuinely pleased for her, he told her that he didn't like feeling abandoned. Sandy had made the shifts endurable. What was he going to do without her?

"You'll find another young woman to joke around with," Sandy assured him, "someone always shows up when you need her."

"If only that were true," Doug replied.

Sandy had insisted that they had to go to the Evergreens, a motel whose lounge a friend had recommended. Drinks were served, congratulations offered, selections made from the jukebox. They tried to talk about other things, but shoptalk had a greater magnetic urgency, not that this bothered her. She relished her new-found detachment.

But Sandy could tell that that she no longer belonged with her former co-workers. That she wasn't really wanted. Now that her life had changed and she had a new job, the others felt as if she'd been rescued and they'd been left behind. Doug bought her another paralyzer, the current favourite among women her age he'd noticed, and she ordered him a beer.

Sipping her drink, smoking one triumphant cigarette after another, she hoped that her real life was now beginning. When the others had left, she took Doug's hands, the first time she'd really touched him, and said she was completely certain that they weren't like other people.

"The true revolutionary must merge her life with the masses," he replied, "I thought you knew that."

Behind him, the many bottles and glasses reflected in the bar's mirror were the glittering, dwarfish spires of benevolent Cambodian temples. They were alive with sympathy.

"Let's pretend we're lovers and rent a room," Sandy offered, "our great date won't last forever."

He'd have to somehow beat his wife to next month's Visa statement, but decided to damn the torpedoes.

"Okay, you're on."

"Tell you what, this one's on me," she said, "because I've never done this before."

Once the door of the motel room was closed behind them the game they'd begun months ago suddenly became unfamiliar. This wasn't accidentally brushing arms in the call centre. This was real. She could feel his erection. His lips kissing her hair. It was finally happening. And yet how could it be? Suspended in their embrace in the middle of the hotel room, they both calculated the dimensions of this strange, this very new situation that they had somehow made for themselves.

"You're so solid," Sandy said, her arms around his shoulders.

"You mean fat," Doug said.

"No, silly, solid. Some men, you touch them, and it's like there's nothing there."

"I've wanted you," Doug stumbled.

"Me too. But it's funny, I feel as though we're being watched. It's important we're here. I think that life is judging us," Sandy said, not exactly sure what she meant. But she sensed that the self-created drama that had brought them there was more valuable and much more unwieldy that mere fucking.

"I think the occasion demands some wine," Doug said "would the lady prefer white or red?"

"Surprise me," Sandy said.

"I can't believe we're alone," Doug said, "let's just savour it a little while."

A full half-hour had passed since room service had brought the wine, and it seemed stupid, humiliating even, for her to be seated on the bed, legs drawn up, him draped sideways over a chair by the window, the way he liked to watch TV at home.

"With this new job, I want to get my own apartment."

"What will your mother think?"

"First, it'll break her heart, but I'm almost twenty-two. Second, it'll break her heart because the original idea was that I should live with her to save up money to go to school."

"Don't you want to go to school?"

"Sure, but look where it got you."

"But this job is only temporary."

"A year's temporary?"

Nothing she could have said or done had the power to push him over to the bed more than this unintentional reminder of where his life had taken him; it opened a canyon inside. But then she pointed her wine glass at him, and he refilled both of their glasses and sat down. His hands were shaking.

"How many women have you slept with?" she asked.

"Only a few, half a dozen, no, five."

"And your wife?" someone she'd only seen picking him up in their car, a woman with nicely borrowed red in her hair.

"About the same."

"Who was the best? Tell me about her."

"Next question."

"If I got my own apartment, would you come and visit me?"

"Would you want me to?"

Sandy got up from the bed, and undressed. The tattoo she'd applied that morning looked real, taking him by surprise.

She watched herself in the bathroom mirror as she took off her earrings and necklace, leaving them beside the sink where she wouldn't forget them. An old boyfriend had always requested that she do this, believing that she was more naked without jewellery.

It wasn't her fault they were still only talking. Maybe he was frightened. She considered opening one of the tiny bottles of shampoo the motel left for its guests, and having a long, invitational shower, but something was wrong and she knew with a fierce certainty that if they ended up in bed together, the ending of the world couldn't astonish her more.

Instead of showering, she stood by the door and looked through the peephole into the contorted world outside their room. Without warning, she opened the door and ran down the hallway past the other rooms. When she returned, the feel of the motel carpet still on her feet, he was clenching her panties, looking dreadful, dazed, as if that moment he'd been suddenly caught stealing.

"I think you should drive me home now," she offered, "don't you?"

"Sandy, I . . ."

As Doug struggled with his orgasm an hour later, he once again felt the hostility in the eyes of the woman at the motel registry. Ancient wrinkled fire. Surely, to her they'd merely been another couple who was going to screw in her motel that night, nothing more. His wife became more delicate, slowed down; he found better, more urgent images; there, finally a tingle from far away that he could focus on. When she was done, his wife came up and kissed him on the mouth, something she always did, and he turned her on her back. She spread her legs happily, but even with his eyes open all he could really see was Sandy's butterfly. It had been alive and ready for him.

Had been, had been alive and ready. For him.

Sandy's keys turning in the lock woke her mother instantly.

"Sweetheart," Liz murmured, reaching for her cigarettes. "What time is it?"

"It's late, Mom, sorry for waking you."

"I wanted to stay up for you. But I fell asleep. Did you have a good time?"

"Yeah. Well, sort of. Not really. It's weird to say goodbye to people you'll never see again. What did you do tonight?"

"Amanda popped by. We watched a movie."

"Amanda gives me the creeps."

"Don't mind her. She means well."

The tiny bottle of shampoo she'd taken from the motel was uncomfortable in her pocket, and for a moment Sandy considered giving it to her mom as a little present, but she didn't want her mother to know she'd been to a motel that night.

The two women sat in the dark, the glow of their cigarettes like two slow fireflies.

Sandy wanted to say *men and women, they just burn each other up inside, don't they?* But if she did, she'd have to tell her mom about Doug. She wanted her mom to confide more about her divorce though she knew her mom would simply say that all of that business was between her and Sandy's father. Sandy was in a slow and quiet space inside; she needed to talk, hear her mom talk.

"Mom?"

"Yes, honey."

"Mom, after all these years, do you ever think of the baby you lost?"

"Sure I do, especially in the summer. Why do you want to know?"

"I don't know. I've just been thinking how she'd be close to my age, meeting men. Just like I am."

"She? Sandy, the baby was a boy. You would have had a little brother. We were going to call him Jeff, not a name your father liked, but he believed that it's a mother's right to name her children. I wanted to call him Jeff because of a boy who lived across from us in the townhouses when you were a baby. He was the most adorable child."

"Are you ever lonely?" Sandy asked.

"Sometimes. But I've got you. My beautiful grown-up baby girl.

"Not so beautiful. And I don't know what it means to be grown-up."

"Amanda tells me not to worry about you, that you'll be fine."

"Amanda's crazy, Mom."

"Aren't we all? Let me tuck you in."

Mother and daughter look at each other, smoke another cigarette, take turns in the bathroom, and then go to bed.

And after Liz and Sandy have fallen asleep, Johnny Cash, from the coffee table, gazes at the pullout sofa bed in the living room, the numerous spider plants, chosen because somebody at work said they clean the air, a goldfish that had arrived in a plastic bag, the half-dozen photos positioned just so in the hallway, the bicycle in the corner, and he recognizes everything for a constricted orchid of betrayal, a song, a dangerous heart of radiance and ruin.

Clouds Aren't Animals

— When he'd gone for a walk a few days after his abdominal surgery, Colin had met a little girl he hadn't seen before down the street. Maybe she was visiting or maybe they'd just moved in that morning. She'd looked to be two, maybe three years old—it's hard to tell at that age. She'd been wearing only her panties, and had placed a rather large and expensive doll on the edge of her family's driveway. The doll was seated, legs splayed on the pavement, looking for all the world as if she'd been put out for the garbage truck to take away. The child was a long way from her doll, and she and Colin had shared a few words together. No one was looking after her. She was wearing purple garden gloves and they chatted about how great gloves are to do things in. A magpie cried way, way above them, but the little girl ignored it, and showed Colin her gloves again.

Telling his friend Norm about the little girl when they sat in the campus pub that night, it wasn't clear to Colin whether there'd been a car in the driveway, though he knew for certain there hadn't been anyone in the living room window keeping an eye out for her. The little girl and her family's lawn contained a tiny, important, and completely irrelevant nugget of the universe, though Colin knew that he would never be able to discover what it was.

As was the case most Saturday nights, the bar was crowded, and happy to open up its heart.

"You'll want to be careful talking about little girls dressed only in their panties," Norm said, still angry over the reception he'd gotten earlier that day when he'd picked up some photos.

The clerk had flashed open his package of pictures and instructed Norm that shots like *these* weren't cute anymore—*these* being some he'd taken of his kids in the bathtub, his daughter about to turn three, his son five.

"No one is going to tell me what I can take pictures of," Norm told the clerk who replied that he was just offering friendly advice, and that it was part of his job, but there was the thrill of power shining from the tall, prematurely balding man's eyes—moist and accusatory.

Colin, who managed a university bookstore, had met Norm years ago when he'd come into the store wanting Colin to stock the current *Prism International* because they'd published a piece of his. Colin told him that he didn't carry literary journals because they never sold and their friendship began when Colin asked him whether he didn't think that there were already enough writers in the world, surely to God no more were needed.

After several drinks, Colin announced that he should have invited his dad to his wedding.

"You didn't invite your own dad to your wedding?"

"I didn't say dad. I meant my grandfather, my dad's dad."

After Colin had told Norm his story about the wedding, Norm asked him whether he liked rum, the Bacardi rum bat insignia above the bar having just caught his eye.

"Colin, I've got a dilemma. Remember that story I had published a few years ago in *Prism*?"

"Tell you the truth, I never read it."

"That's okay, I'm pretty picky about my readers."

"Touché."

"Here's the situation. Remember Marika? My ex? She always thought you were a bad influence."

"She was right."

"She e-mailed me out of the blue about a couple of years ago—it's been ages—and we've been sending e-mails every now and then. She's married again. Anyway, filling her in, I mentioned that story and she wanted to read it. I wasn't sure about sending it, though, because she's in it. And I didn't paint a pretty picture."

"Scandalous."

"Not really. But I don't think she was too happy about it. Because I haven't heard from her since. She won't return my e-mails. It's been a few months now and so I've more or less given up. But here's the rub. I modelled another character in the story on an old friend of mine in Vancouver. His name is Tom. We've been buddies since university, but his character in the story might have been just a little too close to home. And now Tom won't return my e-mails now either. So I figure she got real pissed off with me, somehow got in touch with Tom and told him about the story."

"You think he'd recognize himself? You never told him about it? Maybe they just got tired of your e-mails."

A server swung by and took their order.

"Christ I love a woman's hands."

"Should we invite her to a hotel when the bar closes? Between the two of us we could wake her up a few notches."

"Make her dreams come true."

The music pushed a drunken couple into a table alongside the tiny dance floor, sending a pitcher of beer flying over somebody's leather jacket.

"So what do I do? Do I get in touch with Tom or wait for him to contact me?"

"What are you going to say if he mentions the story?"

"I don't know, I honestly don't know. I had no idea she could be so malicious. Single-handedly she's ruined one of my oldest friendships."

"Well you wrote the story."

"When you have my limited imagination, you write about what passes in front of you. What bugs me is, was she always like that? I mean, if you would've asked me when we were together whether she could do something like this, I would have said no way."

"I always thought she was too good for you."

"No doubt. But Colin this is serious. How do I go back and rethink her? Because she must have had it in her back then; it just never came out. People don't change."

"How do you know?" Colin asked, his interest increasing.

"Life's too short. For most people, it's just, 'huh, what was that?' People can't change Colin because they don't know how to change. And I can't re-imagine her. Trying to refit your memories is like trying to imagine what's at the edge of the universe."

"Here's what you do. Take out an ad. Get a full-page ad in *The Globe* and just say you're fucking sorry. Look at that one."

"Who?"

"The one over there wearing her lingerie and jeans, the one with the stupid boyfriend. While you were in the washroom I wrote her a note. What do you think?"

As he read the note, Norm rolled his head back deep in the laughter that Colin genuinely loved.

"You want to stay for last call?" asks Colin.

"No, I've got to get up and take the kids to the pet store in the morning. Tanya wants a hamster, a pink hamster. Her birthday's coming up. So I've got to get up early."

"You can have one more, just a fast one. Or are you worried about your wife?"

"Some of us Colin," Norm said, clipping the sentence short. "You want a ride?"

"Okay, you win. No, the nurse told me I needed to do some walking. I'll walk home. I like walking at night."

"You're feeling okay?"

"It's not too bad. You go. I'm going to bide my time until the boyfriend takes a piss and then I'll give her the note."

Colin had another scotch, and waited until the woman's boyfriend left her table so he could pass her the note. The walk would help him feel better. To Colin's delight she looked only mildly confused when he tossed the note on the table, and left by the side door. It was very windy. The night was becoming uncomfortably cold.

The note read: *Dear Satan, you're impossible and beautiful and truly terrible, but I could love you all the same.*

Only a few days before, Colin was lying on a cot in an operating room. Breathe deeply, it's pure oxygen, the anesthetist was saying, and because of their odour the man's latex fingers betrayed that he'd stopped for a smoke just before the operation. Colin's own doctor, a plastic surgeon, suddenly appeared from behind and said hello through a mask before turning to his instruments. As he'd expected he would, Colin was having trouble holding his thoughts together. Fastened to a ridiculously narrow cot shaped like a midget cross, with his arms stretched off to the side, feet and chest restrained, he thought of Hollywood's mad scientists and their laboratories. Except that this room held at least two nurses. One relaxed and then captivated him with her voice, and it was very clear—women *were* angels. Luminous creatures only barely hidden beneath flesh that still managed to astonish him. Maybe his surgeon would break open his ribs and fashion him a new woman, an Eve just right for him; but he knew that a body like his would be incapable of producing any miracles.

Just then his mind vanished under the anesthetic, glimpsing as it disappeared a teenager he'd once seen in an airport years before. Tornado warnings had delayed most flights that long day, cancelled others, and hundreds of travellers were frantic to leave Minneapolis behind. And then to the left, twisted in a wheelchair, this young man was being pushed quickly through the crowd in front of Colin. His keening voice, closed eyes, spindly and straying hands indicated his fear. Despite being hurriedly pushed, the young man strained to keep one foot dragging along the floor. Watching that twisted foot in its grey sock move along the floor, Colin sensed the terrified man's desperation; it was if he absolutely had to maintain contact with something solid to shove the chaos away.

Moments after the teenager's image had arrived, bursting across his mind like lightning over parched, instantly shining fields, Colin's unconsciousness registered some pressure on his belly. Some more latex fingers probed and washed recently shaved skin that hadn't been that buttery smooth since boyhood.

As he'd been wheeled into the operating room, crashed through gleaming metal doors that could have led into the kitchen of a luxurious mountain resort, Colin had vowed that if he was to wake up after the operation—and something had told him he would— some weaknesses would have to be burnt away. This promise, which had been made many times before, had then settled on his mind's sleeping surface, floated briefly on its black waves like crepe paper before sinking down beneath along with everything else.

He'd been stranded in the airport for ten hours because his grandfather Patrick had been killed while on a vacation in the States. Thirsty for gin and needing to get some more of the cheap American cigars he'd loved so much, the old man had been making his way to the supermarket when he'd been struck by a car. After the autopsy, the body had been flown home to Ontario and Colin had returned for the funeral.

The driver wasn't at fault, so no charges were laid, which was just as well, Denny, Colin's father, had told him as they drove away from Toronto's airport.

Unsure as to what kind of affection to offer his dad, Colin hadn't touched him at first, but then he embraced him from behind in the parking garage's stairwell. As his dad turned around to meet him, Colin remembered, as usual, just how much bigger a man his dad was.

They'd driven an hour on the busy highway before turning off into the country, the poorly paved road a satisfying and devouring darkness that led to the family cottage. A place into which his dreams often hurled him, a bit of land just a small lawn away from a high, badly eroding bank above a man-made lake, the family cottage was a quick drive from the small town where Colin's dad had grown up. Though he wasn't really a mechanic, Patrick had run a gas station and garage situated at the town's only intersection. Just before the memorial service, Colin learned from his dad that the town's funeral parlor had once been a hardware store. And we lived upstairs, Denny had said—there used to be apartments above the store, probably still are, I suppose it would be quiet to live there now.

Only Denny understood the sardonic eulogy he'd given over his father's closed coffin. As a pallbearer, Colin smelled death for the first time. It smelled yellow, a bleached and yellowy green, something careless. He would try to drink it away that night.

Along with Colin, his aunt and uncle and their families returned to the cottage after the internment, enjoyed the absence of mosquitoes caused by the perpetual wind that came up off the lake, ate some prepackaged lasagna, and then left for their long drives home. It had been the Friday night of a holiday weekend, and sometime after midnight cottagers across the lake started their fireworks early.

"I slept here last night," Denny said as they sat on the porch, "and Dad came in a dream and told me he wanted the cottage back."

"Do you own it now?"

"The will divides it up between the three of us, but I spoke to Kim and Craig tonight and they're willing to let me buy out their shares. No surprise there, they're always broke. He didn't leave much to you, though, just an antique telephone. I don't think he ever forgave you for not inviting him to your wedding. You never really explained."

"But that was centuries ago. What was I supposed to tell him? That I'd never forgiven him for Dale?"

A young Colin has his girlfriend Gina over for dinner.

The electricity's gone off because of a fire in the row houses behind his apartment. They've gone to see the blaze, which has taken over two homes and is threatening a third, but are reassured by a firefighter that Colin's place, across the back alley, is safe. The liquor store a few blocks away is still open, and they buy some tequila on a whim, and drink it in bed.

Colin's bedroom window looks over the alley, but the fire isn't bright enough so they light some candles. There's a door in the bedroom that exits onto a miniature balcony, but it's been nailed shut from the inside, and then painted over.

Colin tells Gina that the balcony, large enough for only one person, is haunted. He's thrilled when she smiles and crosses herself.

It begins to rain. The combination of the rain on the window and the adamant, inquisitive presence of the tequila eventually gives them a rough and ready paradise together on the raft-like bed, so they decide it would be a good idea to get married in the spring.

Colin has a stopwatch from when he used to work out and they play a game of who could bring the other quickest to orgasm. Gina wins. They plan their guest list, but the tequila changes again—it's developing amber talons now—and Colin tells Gina about his grandmother.

She'd died when he was six, the favourite grandson. He hadn't been allowed to go to the funeral, but he remembers his father making trips to the hospital and that it had been during the early autumn because the fall fair had been in town. A heavy woman, a diabetic with a heart condition, Colin's grandmother would often drink Coke while she cradled him on her lap. She would burp, and the two of them would giggle at this apparent transgression of politeness. She made Colin feel adored, and then she was gone. For months he'd dream that he would find her, usually when he was at school, and he would try to bring her back to his parents to show them that they were wrong—Grandma wasn't dead. And he'd been the one who'd found her alive once again. For a few dream seconds he was a hero.

Telling Gina, Colin can still sense his grandmother's presence in a deserted classroom, glowing with afternoon snow and an old January sky, still sharply blue, the air still freezing and unrepentant after all this time.

Years later Colin's mom would tell him that he'd changed after his grandmother had died. His mom would hear him playing in his room, but then she'd realize that he'd been quiet for too long. She'd check on him, and he'd be sitting on his bed, running his fingers through the design knotted on the brown bedspread that once belonged to his grandmother. He'd also been given her shiny tattered wallet, but it hadn't held enough of her to help him. When his mother would ask him what he'd been doing all she could get from him was that he'd been thinking about Grandma.

Only when he'd become a teenager had he understood that his grandfather's second wife, Dale, had been the man's mistress while he'd been married to Colin's grandmother. And his grandmother had known about the affair. He can't wait for me to die, she'd wept to her daughter-in-law decades ago. You'll see, he'll marry her, his grandmother had predicted, and he had, and then even Dale had died.

Touching Colin's ancient grief, the tequila holds it before his eyes, gloating at what it's discovered. When he tells Gina that he refuses to invite his grandfather to their wedding, she quickly sympathizes—a man that loyal to a long-dead grandmother is unlikely to betray his wife, she feels.

"Do you really hold a grudge that long?" Denny asked the night of Patrick's funeral. "Good for you."

"I don't know. Part of me says I was too harsh."

"Well, it means that your sisters get a few thousand dollars each, but you get an antique telephone. It's the one inside, the one on the wall. I'll give you a hundred bucks for it. I'd like to keep it here."

"Sure Dad, okay."

"You're thinking I'm the one who's harsh, aren't you? But there's so much you don't know. Let's say that I can't forgive him, Colin, because he was an uncomplicated and lazy man. The only time he ever really opened up his eyes was when I took him to France."

Colin knew that it wasn't until his retirement years that his grandfather had taken notice of his dad. And he also knew that his dad, the youngest of the three kids, had been the only one who hadn't spent the past few decades twisting money from Patrick.

Denny's dad had taken Patrick to France a few years before. Patrick had been too old to fight in World War II, but he'd known men who'd gone. He wanted to see the D-Day beaches, but wouldn't dare go by himself. They spoke French in France, and Patrick had contempt for Quebec and its catholics. But then he'd been completely unprepared for the generous treatment he received in Normandy. At a family-run restaurant, Patrick and Denny enjoyed an evening with the owners, and had been allowed to stay after the restaurant closed. For two or three hours there'd been free wine, and for Patrick, two delicious cigars.

Patrick had collected pennants from his travels, flown his Ontario flag with pride from an enormous flagpole, coddled his roses in their bed of coca beans, flicked slimy cigar butts on the grass—something that Colin as a barefoot child had learned to avoid—and had gotten into the habit of spending a few weeks in Arizona every year, usually with a different woman. He'd become adept at finding them through newspaper ads but hadn't been entirely successful that year; the woman he'd taken along with him wouldn't have sex so she'd been flown home after two days.

"You had to admire him for his swimming," Denny said, "he swam in the lake every day he could. Before the ice got too thick, he'd break it with a baseball bat. He'd go skinny-dipping. I can still see him going naked down to the lake in November, armed with his baseball bat. It looked like he was setting out to kill something."

"Did you ever go swimming with him?"

"Sometimes."

"Any pictures?"

"No."

"Do you want to go for a swim?"

"Not really."

"The water would be warm. It would do us good."

"I don't like swimming when I'm shit-faced, Colin."

"I admire you Dad, you know that?"

"That must be a nice feeling. I wish I'd admired my father. But I didn't, even when I was a kid. Back then I was simply afraid of him."

"I've never been afraid of you," Colin lied, and noticed the approval on his dad's face. "When did you stop feeling that way about Grandpa?"

"When I realized he was just tedious. Dad was a man who merely reacted to things. He accomplished nothing of value. It's only been in the last few years that we had anything at all to say to each other."

"Well, I'm glad that you're going to keep the cottage."

"It's too bad you live so far away. You and Gina could come and stay for a week or so. You could have the place to yourselves. Except for the weekend, I'd stay in town."

"That was a fucking bizarre eulogy, Dad. I mean, to say that Grandpa deserved death."

"The old man didn't take his life seriously, he had absolutely no idea."

"Who does? Dad, come on."

Sometime later that night Colin and his dad took the boat out. Denny ripped through the thin waves, finally finding the island of sleeping gulls that nestled on the smooth water. He aimed the boat straight through them. And it was as if the birds detonated. Flying up just a small ways into the night sky, they then quickly dropped back into the water, only to be pushed away as the boat continued to cut through them. Offered a turn at steering, Colin shook his head, preferring to watch his father lean into the dark, making the boat curve in ever narrowing counter-clockwise circles.

When Colin came to in the hospital after the operation, he slowly noticed that some of the previously occupied beds were empty, and there was a rubber container attached to his belly, draining blood. He looked around, and pushed himself to stay awake for longer and longer periods, but he also gave in to it, and slept. He registered the time on the clock on the opposite wall, but the space in between his bed and the clock was solid, almost visible, and time couldn't get through.

Eventually a nurse came by and placed his index finger inside a device to measure his pulse. She was surprised that he smoked (*of course he smoked, what did they expect?*) because his pulse was so clear. Doctors and nurses rarely offered good things, but this *is* good news he thought—he'd probably still be able to get a hard-on for a few years longer. Meanwhile his drugged mind was rampant with disconnected images.

He suddenly saw himself vomiting face down in the gravel on the roadside from Trieste to Dubrovnik as a twelve-year-old on a family vacation in Europe. It was like the image pushed itself in front of him, and then disappeared. Colin didn't pay it any attention; he was used to the way his mind lobbed things down at him. But Colin remembered his father helping him up and then telling him to spread gravel over where he'd been sick.

When he was fully conscious, Colin phoned his friend Norm to pick him up and drive him home. It would be at least three weeks until the biopsy results came in, though the doctor was fairly certain that the lipoma wasn't cancerous.

Sitting upright in the car made him glad for the drugs he'd been prescribed, but to make extra sure that he'd sleep Colin had Norm stop by the liquor store so he could buy some scotch. His supply was getting low at home. Norm stayed for one, sent and paid for some Chinese food, and an hour later he stood with Colin in front of the mirror in the bathroom, helping him empty the rubber bag of blood into the sink, and then ordered his friend to bed.

Because of the incision, Colin had to sleep on his back, which took getting used to. Despite the confusion that the drugs caused, he dreamed once more that annoying dream that always placed him in his childhood home, and as always, somehow his old bedroom held a computer, but he couldn't open his e-mail, and it was completely necessary that he find out who'd been writing to him.

The computer kept placing unfamiliar screens in front of him, mazes within even more mazes, and he awoke.

One of the compensations in Colin's life was that he could walk to work. He lived only twenty minutes from the campus, which saved him parking fees and gave him his exercise. Although he'd booked a week off from work to recover from his surgery, he decided he'd go in the next day for a few hours. The line of pain across his belly wasn't too bad, so he got out of bed, made his way down the hall to the loveseat in the living room, and after some channel surfing, realized that the next day was Saturday—he didn't need to go to work.

Because he'd been manager for such a long time the job was easy, but every time he went to work, as soon as the cash registers came into view, he had to step through the sparkling aura of his failure. Instead of running a university bookstore, he should have been a professor. But he'd never been able to finish his doctoral thesis. He'd worked on it for years—years that Gina had put up with the low-paying teaching assistantships—or at least he'd tried to write his dissertation, except that all he'd managed to come up with was the same chapter over and over again. His friends graduated, some found jobs teaching; but in the end he was forced to leave the program. His advisor got him a job at the bookstore, and in due course he'd become manager. When his former professor retired, though, there was no way Colin could force himself to go to the party. There were limits.

He'd turned the bookstore around so it made a profit—the administration loved him—and he kept track of the professors who didn't publish anything. He'd approach them when they came into the store and let them know how delighted he'd be to add something of theirs to the section devoted to university authors.

And every morning when he entered the store he popped a breath mint while that persistent and for some reason coppery inner voice shouted its disappointment in him.

It was closing upon four in the morning, and Colin had just emptied his two bladders once more, swabbed the rubber one, looked at the slightly bloody dressing in the mirror, and glanced briefly at his face. It turned out that codeine went well with scotch. So did cold Chinese food. But then, most things went well with scotch. Except Gina, eventually Gina hadn't gone well with scotch—but that was an old line he'd repeated too often not only to Norm, but also to himself.

From where he sat in the living room he could see the quail eggs.

Inside a thick wooden frame, behind glass, were four spotted eggs hanging in the dark. He'd given them to Gina for her thirtieth birthday, but then one summer he'd crashed into the wall, knocking the eggs off their hook, breaking the one in the lower corner.

He shouldn't have been drunk; he'd been dry for eighteen days, eighteen days and nights that had their own brittle shimmer to them, but that morning he'd been at the Addiction Centre for a physical. They were going to check his liver and kidneys, take some blood, and ask unwelcome questions. But somebody had brought a kid to the waiting room, and this moronic child had shoved his way into the examination room when it'd had been Colin's turn inside. It shouldn't have mattered, but the child's curious gaze at Colin's naked chest caused him to feel greater humiliation than he'd ever felt before and tears began.

He put up with the examination, and honestly answered their questions, and then Gina had found him impossibly drunk when she'd come home from work.

During his first months with naturally blond Gina, before they lived together, he loved to watch her walk down the street heading toward his place for the night, she not knowing that he'd left the apartment to find her in the crowd, to discover her on the wet sidewalks among Portuguese fish markets spilling out of the stores onto the street, and then he'd come up behind her as she rang the doorbell to his apartment.

But that late afternoon, she'd looked at him, and gone to the fridge for a beer, took the time to pour it into a glass, joined him at the messy kitchen table, informed him that this was the last drink they'd ever share together, called her friend Debbie to pick her up, and as he tried to hold her before she went out the door he'd accidentally struck the eggs from the wall.

She hadn't cried until she picked the frame up from the floor and put it back where it belonged. It was his now, she'd said.

He'd promised himself repeatedly that she'd soon return home, but that had been ten, almost ten abruptly inconceivable years ago. Even after she'd taken her things, even after the first year, he'd vowed that Gina would *restore herself to his life again.* And then he at long last had begun learning that she'd made up her mind; she wouldn't be returning. Colin felt deep inside that it wasn't possible for Gina to leave him. But she had.

He was sweating, a little sore from the surgery, and his eyes stung.

The streetlights passed through the curtains, undiminished, as if they were headlights shining a week, maybe a month away in the future, and Colin began to be afraid that he had nothing important in his life anymore.

Colin normally took some vitamins before going to bed, but the nurse in the recovery room earlier that day had told him not to take any Aspirin or any other blood thinners for a few days, so he put the vitamin E back on the shelf above the sink. She'd also said that he should try to walk a few blocks every day so that blood clots wouldn't form in his legs. He'd go for a walk tomorrow, and wear his new shoes.

First he'd go for a walk, and then, why not? he'd drive to a pet store and buy an aquarium; if this insomnia was going to keep at him forever then some fish swimming in the night would give him something to look at. He'd never had time for pets as an adult, but by this time tomorrow the room would glow with fish. The tank would need some decorations so he'd get a mermaid whose nipples blew bubbles.

Setting up a tank turned out to be more complicated than he'd thought. He'd chosen a large one, but he'd been told that he couldn't put fish in it for more than a week, and then he had to proceed slowly, build up the right bacteria, and get sturdy fish first, some dull looking zebras, before he could add any extravagantly coloured ones. The mermaids they sold were pretty tame, so he bought a dragon that rocked and snorted bubbles instead, the standard stones, and a bag of fetching turquoise skulls, each the size of a child's fingernail, and then some blue, green, and purply-black plastic plants. At the till, he asked if someone could help him put the tank in his trunk because he'd recently had surgery.

The young woman who'd hoisted everything into his car asked him if he was going to have help when he got home. He told her immorally appealing face that he had a strapping wife at home who would give him a hand.

Colin was careful driving home. He'd lost some driving points two years before when, waiting at a traffic light, he'd drunkenly mistaken a full moon for the signal to advance into the intersection.

He'd ask the kids across the street if they'd help him. Madison, the oldest, cut his lawn each summer; Colin would give him ten bucks, and his two younger sisters five apiece. It would give them something to do, and Lord only knew that they could use the money.

The kids washed the stones in his licorice-red colander, splashed so much water on the floor that he'd had to throw down a bunch of towels, and after an hour's sloppy work, they joined him for a beer, pop, and smoke break. Michelle, the five-year-old, started crying when she dropped the ceramic dragon on the floor, breaking off its head, but it didn't matter: she could take it home and surprise her dolls. After all, how many Barbies had their own dragon's head? The kids' excitement was like a bank of fog hovering just above their heads; Colin hoped that they would remember that afternoon for the rest of their lives.

He took some more Tylenol and placed the alarm clock on the coffee table; Norm had phoned when the kids had been there and they'd agreed to meet at the student bar at ten that night if Colin was up to it. He closed the curtains, and fell asleep on the couch next to the satisfying sound of the fish tank's pump.

Even though he felt only slightly drunk, Colin was careful as he walked from the student bar. The night's cold sobered him a little, but it wasn't a night to stay out for very long. He was glad that his house wasn't far away. Clouds aren't animals, but those tearing across the blackened sky that night could have been enormous marine creatures, a ghostly herd sweeping just beneath the ocean's surface, a fine black line just above them that held the faintest smudge of blue. Stars bit through this ocean, and Colin was swaying as he looked above him, taking in the stars, swaying, almost falling, when he was struck very hard from behind.

The blood from his face after hitting the sidewalk told him that the scrape was serious. Even within his fear Colin noted that the scrape would easily last until next week when he had to return to work, which would be embarrassing, but worse, one of the arms had broken off his glasses.

If he'd known about Colin's surgery, Satan's boyfriend might not have continued kicking the way he did. Finally, he picked up the older man's glasses and threw them way, way off into the snow.

A young woman found the glasses on Monday morning, thought about taking them to the lost and found office, but decided to place them on a nearby bench. Anyone who'd broken their glasses would try to find them where they'd originally been lost. But she couldn't understand why they were there in the first place. It didn't make much sense. The lenses were so thick—whoever owned the glasses would have needed them and known immediately that they'd been damaged.

Sometimes the Heart Vomits Sand,
Sometimes It's Bathed in Light

— My wife and I get the newspaper delivered, and I normally read it at night, but one day last July I decided to take the morning off, take the paper with me, and just amble around downtown. I paid some utility bills, and bought a watch in a sidewalk sale at the mall. Its plastic band was blue–green, like ocean waves, though it was its face—a poorly executed theft of Salvador Dali's melting clocks—that convinced me to buy it. I wandered around the lake after joining the mall people, mostly senior citizens who spend their mornings holding forth in the food court. Much to my surprise, almost none of them were wearing slip-on shoes.

It had rained earlier—none of the park benches were dry—so I ended up sitting on the business and sports pages, subject matter that bores me, though I wish I could take an interest in sports at least. The air that morning offered its gifts, as only the prairie after a thunderstorm can.

Because my eyes were sore, I just dipped into the newspaper. Looked at the seagulls. But then I brought the paper up close. A passport-sized photo showed a young woman, probably on her graduation day. Most people in grad shots look dreadful. It's as if the very second the camera flash goes off, the sudden light sentences them to a lifetime of forgetfulness. What you get in the developed picture is their unconscious, slow leap between resistance and then consent to such a judgment. But this woman was different. I couldn't tell whether she'd taken the formal occasion seriously—but for that day at least and almost certainly longer, she owned whatever space surrounded her.

I'd been flipping through the pages when this woman's face drew me, offering an instant's width of sexual curiosity that immediately dissolved because the photograph headed an obituary column. And the grad photo was misleading. The person in the picture was in her early twenties, but apparently she'd died a grandmother. There was something unfair in taking that youthful moment and using it, truly a lifetime later, to announce her death in a public place.

Innumerable greys gathered overhead. I don't know whether other people pay much attention to clouds, but that morning, the sky held darts of light that glimmered like vodka does after it's been kept in the freezer.

Barely moving, monumental, the clouds made me think of classic black and white photography. The sky could have been a vast picture of one of those massive apartment buildings that close on so many Parisian boulevards. Several floors high, narrow balconies pressed up against the wall's rough skin, the roof a slanting, perfect line of chimney pots. And then, while no one's paying attention, one of the windows bursts, abruptly blazes out a flaming shower of magnesium away from the stained bricks, and then it's dark again, the burst of light's disappeared, harming no one.

I returned to the obituary column. It isn't accurate to say that my desire for her stopped when I realized she was dead, because I registered that there was no mention of a bereaved husband. Whoever wrote the obituary had omitted her date of birth or age at death. A gleam of envy for her children's father slid next to something inside me—a sense of fleeting, irrational grief? I'm not sure. Had I been present when she'd turned toward the photographer—an impossibility because of the difference in our ages—I could easily have fallen in love with this woman, but perhaps I have—her face is a version of my wife's, only more radiant.

It began to rain again, really pour, so I went home, tossed the mostly unread paper on the pile of newspapers I keep to eventually read, then continued into a day that I can no longer recall. But that night I clipped the column and used it for a bookmark well into the autumn, her image and life's story accompanying me through eight or nine novels. But then I lost the clipping somewhere.

After a late dinner, my wife stays upstairs watching her crime dramas, and I go downstairs into my study. I usually read, surf the Net, mostly checking out the live sites. Then I like to breeze through the previous week's newspapers, before going outside around midnight for my regimen of two glasses of red wine, the day's final cigarettes. Stare at the trees, the dark lawn, or snow, depending upon the season. No doubt something's different each night, though I'm certainly not perceptive enough to notice things like that. I return to the same old things, wonder why one thinks of this over that, let the day's emotions sink beneath the night, and then, sometimes reluctantly, head to bed. Undress in the dark, and upon entering the bed, reach up to touch the wooden headboard to ward off the bad. And then, plummet like a stone. When morning arrives, the new day strikes me as something I'd forgotten about, a little like encountering a song on the radio that you hadn't heard since you were a teenager.

From a distance, the woman's picture in the clipping showed how she would age; the teeth would take over the face and shadows on her neck would become cords of skin. But at just the right position, about six inches, her face took over; something in it shone even though her skin was only newsprint.

I didn't know her. She was just someone in the newspaper, not even a ghost. I used a magnifying glass to see her better, which pulled the black-bordered columns detailing other deaths closer to her. Up close, the photo's black dots opened from her face like pores. She'd had three children whom she'd taught, according to the column, that being afraid of anything was a crime. It was after the cremation—she would be ash by now—but her youthful face in the photograph projected confidence. A dogged, rebellious innocence. She looked as though she'd been devout in her early life, but then a beguiling intricacy would have emerged as she aged. Apparently, she'd travelled a great deal. Instead of flowers, people were advised to give to a charity I didn't recognize.

I wondered if she'd ever swayed with her children at the top of a Ferris wheel, children who now had kids of their own. What was she like when she was caught up in the blurry exactitude of the day-to-day? A woman of her generation would have given birth without her husband accompanying her—how had those long hours passed? Did she have any favourite foods? Would she have been able to say what her best moments had been?

My favourite stories are those that ask: what does it mean to love someone?

Sometimes the heart vomits sand. Sometimes it's bathed in light.

Once when my wife was lonely for me across that distance in which I seem to live, I took a helium-filled balloon, left over from a party the night before, and tied the string to one of her toes. Then I made pornographically exact, and then finally generous and jubilant love to her, the balloon going crazy, and all the while she cried in more voices than anyone could be expected to understand. This happened years ago—do I have the nerve to ask her if she remembers that late Sunday afternoon at all? And even if she does, what am I supposed to say to her?

But you, my newspaper lady bordered in black, something tells me that you know all of these things and more.

Your obituary says that you died after a long illness.

I've found the clipping again; well, to be accurate, the new cleaners discovered it when they finally made headway in my study. Now I know your name once more, and where you lived.

And you know what? You wouldn't believe it, but, on an impulse, I phoned your son Malcolm yesterday. I told him I didn't want him to think I was a ghoul, reminding him of his dead mother after all these months. I fudged, and told him that I'd been going through old newspapers and read about you, and that I wanted to express my regrets. I told Malcolm that even though I'd never met his mother, she sounded as though she was a gift to the world. After the initial awkwardness, we agreed that you were a truly extraordinary lady, and after an hour on the phone, we discovered that we're more or less the same age. Then our differences began to emerge, as they will, so we said goodbye. He did mention, though, that he had one regret: the family video he'd made and shown you during your last summer.

I imagine you in a housecoat watching the video on the television. You're with your family, surrounded by the plants you love. Malcolm had shot the video earlier in the summer; within the video you're sitting on the grass bank, watching your family on the dock at your son's cottage. There they all are, throwing stones off the dock into the lake. Then the video camera's passed to someone else. You can see the wooden platform rocking every time a boat goes by.

Suddenly, your son jumps from the dock onto the grass, his hair and suede jacket making him look like a used car salesman stranded in the '70s, and he picks up a stick, yells that it's a snake, and throws it to your grandson Peter who calmly tosses it back into the waves. Golden haired, still wearing sleepers to bed, and he's already caught on to his father's antics.

Malcolm told me that later that morning you'd gone into your bedroom and you wouldn't let anyone come in to see what was the matter. But he's convinced that you were upset because when you saw the video, it was as if you saw your family the way they would be after you were gone. It's the one thing he wishes he could change.

I can see his point; the video only contains seconds of you, so it *would* be like seeing your family from the grave. But I suspect that what drove you into your bedroom after seeing the video was something only you could understand.

When you'd first been diagnosed, you'd been astonished by the sheer wildness of the news, the way it seized you so fiercely. It wasn't that you were afraid of dying, that wasn't it at all, fear is familiar. It was something else that gripped you at all hours of the day, only rarely, so terribly rarely letting you be. Because that was part of it—you couldn't be you anymore.

That people treated you differently took some getting used

to, but that was possible to accommodate; it even made a kind of weird sense. Why shouldn't the living perceive the chronically ill as fundamentally different, even lesser than themselves?

But this news about dying was much worse than having to adjust to their careful words. It was as if some force had hurled you terrifyingly away from all that existed, into some alien, shifting place, and yet simultaneously condemned you to live in the actual world.

Death stole from you, made your very being fraudulent somehow. And then, gradually, you learned that your memories could form a temporary defence. And this is why the video was so terribly unfair.

I can see you so clearly.

It's not that you didn't recall that morning on the dock from earlier in the summer, you did and you didn't, though that business with the stick you'd completely forgotten. It's not that your memory is particularly faulty. Everyone knows memory's lapses. No, this business with the family video is entirely unnatural.

Watching the videotape took you by surprise.

Because it was so vivid, so full, so monumentally dense with detail. The video holds every syllable your grandson Peter uttered, each shimmery inch of every wave that went by. Every creak of the dock, even the algae's there for everyone to see. And all you had within your skull were some badly scratched images, perhaps less than a dozen left over from that entire week spent at the cottage. An entire week and that's all that remained.

The knowledge of how little you actually held threatened to gut you. For the first part of that afternoon, locked away in your bedroom, the video cursed you into the poverty of your own life, something the disease had failed to do.

But then some strength returned.

If the video made the present narrower than any window ledge, you would play with the future. You dug up your calligraphy pen and wrote a note to Peter your grandson, telling him how proud you were of him. Along with some money, you would give him some lines penned by a woman that he probably wouldn't even remember.

And then, the best part. You rooted around in your closet to find a box.

Years ago, you couldn't resist an alarm clock you'd seen in China. It was rusty now, but on its face you can still see a crowd of youthful revolutionaries. Up near ten o'clock Mao laughs in celebration. The second hand is a grey airliner that, when the clock is wound up, flies in a circle 'round the hours.

The clock's special sign of absurd genius? The upraised fist of a young woman in pigtails serves to mark the seconds themselves. As each second passes, her salute ticks back and forth. Her moving hand is so ridiculous it's brilliant. The other cadres' faces are a muted sandy brown, the colour of a paper bag. The Great Helmsman has been fleshed out more fully, his teeth still sparkle, and his cheeks dance with light.

You removed the glass face on the clock, took a marker and coloured in Mao's teeth, gave him a dandy mustache. And an earring. Next you put everything in the box—the note, the clock, and the marker—and wrapped it up in newsprint. Then you wrote on the top that it was a special gift for little Peter from Grandma, to be his when, across the years, he'd eventually become a man.

Acknowledgements

I would like to thank Thomas Wharton, my editor at NeWest Press, for his endless patience, wise suggestions, and eagle eye. Friends over the years offered encouragement and advice. Thomas Bredohl, Derek Brown, John Chaput, Joanne Gerber, Britt Holmström, Ken Mitchell, Jeff Pfeifer, and Kathleen Wall—you all have my gratitude. A special thank you to Amy Snider for inspiring the collection's title story. I would like to say a special thank you to Pico Iyer who kindly gave me permission to cite from an article he wrote on Leonard Cohen. Finally, I wish to express my deep admiration for (and appreciation to) Susan Lohafer, short story theorist and close reader extraordinaire: I've learned so much from you.

The following stories have been previously published, but appear here edited for this collection.

"Fathers, Sons." *Grain.* 32.3 (Winter 2005): p. 45–8.

"Angels." *The Harpweaver.* 10 (Spring 2002): p. 26–38.

—Also Shortlisted for *THIS Magazine* Fourth Annual Great Canadian Literary Talent Hunt. (1 August 2000)

"But Then the Uncanny Put Its Hand on My Knee." *Prairie Fire.* 22.2 (Summer 2001): p. 4–12.

—1st Place *Prairie Fire*'s 2000 Fiction Contest.

"Writing Letters to Those You Love." *Queen Street Quarterly.* 2.2 (Summer 1998): p. 8–15

MICHAEL TRUSSLER was born in Kitchener, raised in New Hamburg, ON, and currently lives in Regina, SK. He received a BA and MA in English Literature from York University and a PHD from the University of Toronto, completing his doctoral thesis on the contemporary American short story. In 1997, Trussler began teaching English courses on American literature, literary theory, and the short story at the University of Regina. He has published book reviews, literary criticism, poetry, and short fiction. Trussler has also won three teaching awards, and is the Chief Editor of *Wascana Review*. He has travelled widely in the United States and Europe, is a father of two, an amateur photographer, and has a fascination with visual art.